Mystery in Rocky Mountain National Park

National Park Mystery Series: Book 1

Aaron Johnson

ILLUSTRATED BY
The Author

COVER ILLUSTRATION BY
Anne Zimanski

HTTPS://NATIONALPARKMYSTERYSERIES.COM

Cover Artwork by Anne Zimanski

Illustrations by Aaron Johnson.

This is a work of fiction. Names, characters, organizations, historical events, and incidents are the products of the author's imagination. The roles played by historical figures and organizations in this narrative and their dialogue (while based on the known facts of their real lives) are also imagined. The marmot in chapter sixteen, however, is a real marmot (his name is George Montgomery Towns), and he is portrayed as himself and was in no way harmed in the writing of this book.

Paperback ISBN: 978-0-9897116-5-4

Ebook ISBN: 978-0-9897116-6-1

To Jenah, India, and Zion.

"It all turns on affection."

- Wendell Berry
Jefferson Lecture, 2012

CHAPTER 1

SUMMER 1880 – SOMEWHERE NEAR ESTES PARK, COLORADO

"Sir, I've got the boy locked up in the tack shed."

"Who is he?" asked the older man.

"Don't know, Sir. Looks about sixteen, seventeen, maybe. He don't resemble any of the families in these parts."

"What exactly did he see, Ted?"

"He seen me burying it down by the creek, Sir."

The older man looked upset. He pinched the end of his gray mustache and stared at the shed with narrowed eyes.

Inside, the boy was frantically searching for a way to escape. He had tried the door, but it was latched from the outside. He turned his attention to the two windows, which faced west, where a blood-red sun was sinking behind the Rocky Mountains.

I've been here less than twenty-four hours and already found trouble, he thought to himself as he pulled on the frame of the first window. It wouldn't budge. *Must be nailed in place.* Through the panes of wavy glass, he could see the two men outside, just ten paces from the small barn that held him. He recognized the first man, the one who had locked him up. He wore leather boots, dust-covered denim jeans, a white shirt, and a cowboy hat. The ranch hands who'd chased the boy down had called him "Boss." But this was the first time he had seen the older man. He was tall, and wore a gray, woolen suit, the kind he had seen rich gentlemen wear back in the city. The jacket half concealed a dark vest, and a bowler hat covered the man's thinning silver hair. He pulled a pocket watch from his jacket and flipped it open. Its gold surface gleamed in the fading sunlight. Then he drew a thin-framed set of spectacles from the breast pocket of his jacket, put them on, and read the dial. Seeing this, the boy's heart, which was already racing, began to slam against his ribcage. *I don't have much time. They're deciding what to do with me.*

He pushed on the second window. It slid on the wood track.

But to leave now would be foolish. The men would see him the instant he slipped through the window, and with the horses so close by, the ranch hands would quickly lasso him into the dirt, just as they had done down by the creek.

He scanned the walls. They were covered with bridles, saddles, and coils of weathered gray rope. He looked up into the rafters, and the idea came to him in a flash.

While the men looked away, he gently slid the window frame along the track until it was open. He bent down and furiously untied his right boot, then scraped its mud-caked sole along the white paint of the windowsill. He put the boot back on, climbed into the rafters, and lay down. There he would wait.

CHAPTER 2

PRESENT DAY – OHIO

Jake's dad woke him before sunrise. "Time to get going."

"Dad, what time is it?" Jake asked, rubbing his eyes.

"4 AM. I want us to get on the road before the traffic starts."

"This is cruel and unusual punishment."

"You're right. It's cruel and unusual," his dad replied and flicked on the light. "But it's not punishment."

Jake squinted and shielded his eyes from the light. "Sure feels like it."

"Grandma has breakfast for you. If you want, you can sleep more while we drive."

After changing out of his PJs and into jeans and a t-shirt, Jake Evans ambled down the creaky stairs of his grandparents' old farmhouse, drawn by the scent of bacon and waffles. Moonlight streamed through a window, illuminating the framed photographs on the wall. There must have been over a hundred of them. Jake stopped to study his favorite. It was taken just two years ago on Jake's eleventh birthday. In the photograph, Grandpa Evans wrapped his arm around Jake, who held the long handle of a shovel in his hands. Beside them was the apple tree they had planted, and behind them were twenty more trees just like it. Jake's eyes were drawn to the smile on his grandpa's face, and he was overcome by an unexpected wave of emotions. Warmth and confidence swirled inside his chest as he remembered that day and what it was like to plant the orchard with his grandpa. And there was sadness, the kind that tries to steal all the good memories away.

About six months ago, a few days after Thanksgiving, Jake's grandfather had died. Kidney failure. And complications. Jake didn't like that word, "complications." He pushed those memories out of his mind and stared at the photograph, hoping the image of that day in the orchard would replace them.

Jake and his mom and dad were spending only one night at his grandma's house before their long drive to Colorado. Mr. Evans, Jake's dad, wanted to check on her before leaving on their vacation. They would be gone for the next two months, traveling to ten different national parks.

Jake walked through the hallway and living room and into the kitchen, where his grandma stood at the stove. At seventy-nine years old, his grandmother could still hear footfall in the kitchen over the sound of crackling bacon.

"You want your eggs fried or scrambled?" she asked.

"Scrambled. Thanks, Grandma." He sat down at the table, and his grandma placed a plate full of steaming waffles in front of him.

"You've got a big day ahead of you. Sounds like you three are driving straight through to Colorado."

Jake nodded, his mouth full of waffles.

She leaned toward him and studied his face. "Either you're just tired, or there's something else going on." She went back to the stove and then asked, "Your mom said the school year didn't end so great."

"Mom tells you everything, doesn't she?"

"Most things. At least the things that matter."

Jake's grades were fine. The basketball season was okay. But things were not okay with Gabe and Alex. The three of them had been close friends for years. Then something had happened. Jake couldn't quite understand what, but like a canoe you forget to tie up at night, they had drifted away from each other. The lunchtime conversations had changed. Gabe and Alex were into gaming now—something Jake didn't care much about. Their words were like a foreign language, and he felt like he was looking in from the outside. Every now and then, Gabe and Alex would eat at another table. Then one day, Jake looked up and realized he was eating alone.

Then Nick disappeared. At least that's how it seemed to Jake. Last Fall, his brother moved an hour away for his first year of college. When Nick came home on the weekends, Jake forgot about feeling so alone. Then Nick got busy with classes and college stuff, and the weekend visits stopped. It was like Nick had evaporated.

Then grandpa died.

No friends, no Nick, no Grandpa.

He poked at his waffles. "Just missing Grandpa, I guess."

His grandma sat down at the kitchen table across from him and reached out her hand. "I bet you do, Jake. As strange as it sounds, that's a good thing. It hurts. But it says a whole lot about how much you loved him and how much he loved you."

Jake squeezed her hand, nodded, and tried to smile.

"Your Grandpa left you something."

Jake put down his fork and watched her walk across the room to a drawer. She pulled it open, drew something out, then came back to the table and slid a small note across its wooden surface. In his grandpa's handwriting, the envelope read "Jax." It was the nickname his grandpa had given him. Jake carefully opened the envelope and pulled out a piece of paper.

Dear Jax,

 Always try to inspire curiosity.

 Seek help early. Learn from friends.

 Now, understand, my boy, every real treasure exploits neglect.

 The adventure begins,

 Grandpa.

Dear Jax,

Always try to inspire Curiosity.
Seek help early. Learn from Friends.
Now understand, my boy,
every real treasure
exploits neglect.
The Adventure Begins,
Grandpa

"*That's strange,*" Jake whispered to himself.

Jake sighed, and his shoulders fell. All he wanted wa
another adventure with his Grandpa. Instead, he had lei
Jake a confusing and sappy list of advice.

He read it again.

Then it struck him. How could he have missed it? A null cipher! It wasn't the first time his grandpa had written him a note in code. Like this note, most of his birthday cards had been some kind of puzzle.

Jake grabbed a pencil that lay on the table and began to underline the first letter of each word of the first line.

Always try to inspire curiosity.

He assembled the letters: A T T I C.

Then the second line:

Seek help early. Learn from friends.

S H E L F F

The third:

Now, understand, my boy, every real treasure exploits neglect.

N U M B E R T E N

"So, what does it say?" his grandma asked, placing the eggs and bacon on his plate.

"It's a code," Jake replied.

His grandma smiled. "That figures. It's just like your grandpa to do something like that."

"It says, Attic, Shelf F, Number 10."

His grandma walked across the room again, pulled a key from a key rack, and handed it to Jake. "Finish your breakfast first."

Jake scarfed down the rest of his food, grabbed the key,

and ran back through the house and up the stairs to the top floor. He nearly collided with his parents who were carrying their overnight bags down the stairs.

"Whoa," his dad said as Jake rushed past. "The sloth I woke up has changed into a squirrel."

"Sorry," he called back. "I've got to find something before we leave."

"Make it quick. I want to be on the road in ten minutes."

At the attic door, Jake slid the key into the lock, opened it, and pulled on a dangling string to switch on the light. He raced up the attic stairs into a large open space filled with old trunks and furniture. Clothing on hangers hung from pipes set through the rafters, and nails poked their spiked ends through the ceiling, holding the shingles onto the roof.

Across the room, under a tall dormer window, Jake spied a desk surrounded by bookshelves and piled with stacks of papers. On its surface sat a ham radio. A thick wire ran from the back of the radio up into the rafters, where it zig-zagged across them, turning the entire ceiling into a giant antenna. Wires snaked through holes in the attic walls and ran outside into the big oak trees that surrounded the house. Jake recalled how his grandpa used to come up here at night and talk with people on the radio from all over the country. It was kind of old-fashioned, but Jake thought it was cool.

"Shelf F," Jake muttered to himself, scanning the bookshelves. None of them were labeled. He stood back and stared for a while. Then it came to him. Jake counted the shelves from left to right. There were twenty-six, the exact number of letters in the alphabet. Working top-to-bottom and left-to-right, he found what he hoped was shelf F and began looking for book number ten. But there were only nine books.

"Jake!" his mom's voice called up the stairs. "We've got to go!"

"Okay, I'll be right down."

He bent down, picked up book number 9, and opened

it to the title page—*The Journals of Lewis and Clark.* There was nothing special about it. Most of the books were history books like this one. Jake sat down on the floor and placed it back on the shelf. That's when something unusual caught his attention—faint writing on the back panel of the bookcase behind the books on shelf F. He laid down on his belly to examine it. Though he could barely make it out, it was without a doubt the number ten. Jake reached out his hand, pressed on the panel, and it swung open at this touch. He reached further inside and felt the rough leather surface of a book. He drew it out, sat up cross-legged on the floor, and blew the dust off the cover.

It was bigger than a normal book and older and thicker than anything on the bookshelves. The leather cover was dyed black, and the front was embossed with a large decorative letter E. He opened it to the first page, which revealed another note, also in his grandfather's handwriting.

As Jake went to open the note, his dad's voice called up the attic stairs. "Jake! Now! It's time to go!"

Jake slipped the paper back into the book and hurried down the stairs, grabbed his bag from the guest room, and made his way back to the kitchen. His parents were already in the truck. Jake said a quick goodbye to his grandma and gave her a hug.

"Take care of that." She nodded toward the book. "He's given you his most prized possession."

CHAPTER 3

THE SCRAPBOOK

J ake settled into the backseat of the truck and was soon overtaken by sleep. He woke up in a flat landscape where the sun was rising, its red light illuminating the fog that rose like steam from the newly planted fields. Telephone poles flashed past the window at a steady beat as Jake blinked his eyes and stretched.

"Where are we?" he asked his parents in a raspy voice.

"Western Illinois," his dad replied. "We'll stop soon, just after we cross into Missouri."

Twenty minutes later, they pulled off the interstate. While his dad fueled the truck, Jake and his mom went inside the convenience store. Jake got some beef jerky, peanut M&Ms, a snack bag of his favorite chips, and some chocolate milk. It was road-trip food at its best.

As they pulled back onto the highway, Jake popped

some M&Ms in his mouth, opened the scrapbook, and drew out the note.

Jax,

This record of our family's adventures is now yours. Keep it safe. You will want to begin on page twenty-seven, photo number two.

Grandpa

He started at the front, turning pages and counting. It was a scrapbook full of pictures. When he got to page 27, his eyes scanned the photos. The first showed a broad meadow where a herd of elk grazed. A winding creek cut through the valley, and snow-capped mountains loomed in the distance. The second photo was of a cabin. Its stone base was built to shoulder height, and wood siding covered the rest of the building. The cabin had a chimney made of the same rock as the stone steps leading to its front door.

Jake was confused. Why would his grandpa want him to turn to a photo of some old building?

Then he noticed how all of the photos were held to the pages of the scrapbook with small, white, triangular mounts. Carefully, he slipped the photo out of the mounts, turned it over, and found writing on the back. It read:

Radio Transmission November 22nd, 2018: Meet Jasper here in RMNP the week of May 28th

"Hey, Dad, what's RMNP stand for?"

"It's where we'll be tonight. Rocky Mountain National Park. Just like your grandpa planned."

"What do you mean? I thought you and mom planned this vacation."

"We didn't. A few years back, I told your grandpa that I wanted to take a couple of months off work so our family could vacation in the national parks. Since he had spent years visiting all of them, I asked if he would pick some of his favorite places for us. He mapped this entire trip out, reserved our campsites, everything."

Jake's dad looked back at him through the rear-view mirror. "Grandma said you were looking for something he left for you. Did you find it?"

Jake held up the scrapbook for them to see.

His dad looked at its image in the rearview mirror. "I wondered what had happened to that old thing. It's a scrapbook, a journal of all your grandpa's travels to see the national parks. From the time he was your age, he would visit them whenever he could. And when they created a new park, he would go off to see it. I believe all sixty-two are in there. You might find some pictures of me and your Aunt Caroline from trips we took as a family."

Jake turned toward the back of the scrapbook and found a photo of his dad and aunt standing with his grandma and grandpa in front of a sign that read *Acadia National Park*. Across the page were more faded color photographs of an island with ships in the harbor. Flipping through the pages toward the front, the photos went from color to black-and-white. His grandpa became a younger man. Several pages later, a boy appeared in a photo—a boy who looked exactly like Jake, except perhaps a couple of years older.

"Can I see it?" his mom asked.

Jake passed it through the opening between the front seats to her. She leaned forward and examined the picture. "Do you know who this boy is, Honey?"

Jake's dad glanced at the photo. "I believe that's my great-grandfather. And the man standing beside him is his dad." He looked at Jake in the rearview mirror. "Your grandpa collected most of what you'll find in there, but it goes back several generations."

His mom passed the scrapbook back to Jake, and he

looked at the photo again. Mountains filled the background, and just behind the boy hung a long, cloth banner that read: Rocky Mountain Nat'l Park Dedication, Sep. 4. 1915.

"Grandpa left a note inside," Jake said. "It says to begin on page twenty-seven at a photo of some old cabin. And there's a note on the back."

Jake passed the photograph up to his mom and dad.

Seeing the photo and the note, his dad laughed. "That's just like your grandpa. Jake, I think that might be the first clue for a scavenger hunt."

"What do you mean?"

"Well, when your aunt and I were kids, your grandpa would write clues for us and hide them. Each clue gave directions to the next clue until we found the treasure at the end. It appears he's done the exact same thing for you."

Jake held the scrapbook on his lap, stunned by what he'd just heard and feeling it soak in. His grandfather had planned this trip, taking them into places like the Grand Canyon, Yosemite, and Yellowstone. And he had hidden clues to create a scavenger hunt stretching over thousands of miles of wild places, through lands filled with waterfalls tumbling over massive cliffs, where windswept sand dunes met snow-capped mountains, immense canyons stretched beyond the horizon, and forests of ancient redwood trees reached to touch the clouds. A scavenger hunt in the most beautiful and rugged places on earth.

His dad's voice interrupted his thoughts. "Well, it looks like your summer just got a lot more interesting. When we get to the park, you can show a ranger that photo of the cabin. Someone will know where it is."

"Thanks, Dad."

"You know," his mom said, "Wes and Amber will be joining us sometime tomorrow. Maybe you could ask them to help you out?" Wes was Jake's younger cousin, and Amber was the daughter of his parent's friends, the Catalinas. For years, his parents had talked about the three families vacationing together. So, last summer, when they were making plans, they had invited the Catalinas and Wes's family to join them.

"Um, I think I'd rather keep this to myself right now." Jake didn't like how protective his words had sounded. But this new connection with his grandpa was something special, and telling everyone about it just didn't feel right.

His mom turned around in her seat. "Well, I know your cousin loves figuring things out. He'd really enjoy it."

"Mom, I said, I just don't want to share it right now."

"Okay. You don't have to, but I'd like you to keep open to the idea."

He sighed and mumbled, "Alright. I will."

Jake's curiosity led him to examine the two other

black-and-white photos on the page. He pulled the second photo out of its mounts and flipped it over. The back was blank. The third photo was of a mountain landscape. He tugged at it, but it wouldn't budge. He didn't want to tear it, so he let it be. Something was different about this one; its middle bulged, curving away from the page.

Jake pressed down on the photo with his finger and could feel something hidden underneath. Sliding his fingernail along the edge, he lifted the bottom of the photograph, and the corner of a small envelope slid out. He pinched it and pulled out perhaps the smallest envelope he had ever seen. He opened the flap and tapped the mouth of the envelope against the palm of his hand. Nothing came out. Holding it up to the light, Jake looked inside. *Why would my grandpa put hide an empty envelope in here?* Then something caught his eye. The lightest script, in pencil, was written along the inside. Jake tore the envelope open and read the message: Find the Old Man of the Mountain. He'll show you the way.

That's weird. I wonder if the Old Man of the Mountain is the Jasper guy I'm supposed to find?

He filed the message away, tucked the envelope back in its secret spot, and closed the scrapbook. Jake leaned his head against the window and watched the trees go by, thinking about the clues he'd just found and imagining where these next two months might take him.

Night came slowly as they drove in the direction of the westering sun. They crossed the Colorado state line, greeted by a roadside sign that read: *Welcome to Colorful Colorado*. Jake expected to see mountains. Instead, he stared out at endless miles of prairie grasses bending in the wind.

He had almost fallen asleep again when the city lights of Denver appeared. An hour later, the orange glow of the city gave way to the darkness of the foothills. They were following a winding road through the night when Jake's dad brought the truck and camp trailer to a complete stop on the highway. The truck lights revealed the shape of a massive animal standing in the road.

"Whoa!" Jake leaned forward and stared at the creature. "That thing is the size of a horse! Is that an elk?"

"Sure is," his dad replied.

It was early in the year, but the animal's antlers were already an impressive sight, growing high and wide above its head.

"The male elk are called 'bulls,'" his dad explained. "And this guy is a big one."

Jake's dad put his flashers on so any vehicles behind

him would know to slow down. The bull elk sauntered across the highway and was soon followed by seven smaller ones, including two tiny elk still with their spots.

His dad pointed out the windshield. "Those smaller ones in the middle are *cows*; that's what you call a female elk. Can you guess what they call the babies?"

"Well, if the males are *bulls* and the females are *cows*, the babies are probably called *calves*," Jake answered.

"Bingo." His dad replied.

The animals crossed the road and faded into the forest. Mr. Evans turned off the truck's flashers and drove forward into the night. "This also means we're getting close. A couple thousand elk live around Estes Park. Seeing these guys means we'll be in the town soon."

"Estes Park? Is that different from Rocky Mountain National Park?"

"Yes," his dad replied. "Rocky Mountain National Park is a *park*. Estes Park is a *town*."

"Well, that's confusing. If it's a town, why do they call it a park?"

"Back when the settlers came from the East into the mountains," his dad explained, "they looked for open valleys to raise livestock and plant crops. They called those big open places *parks*. So, the town got its name from the valley where it was established."

At that moment, they passed a sign that read: Entering

Township of Estes Park, Colorado. Elevation 7522'.

Jake did the math in his head. His hometown in Ohio was only a thousand feet above sea level. A mile is 5,280 feet. That meant they had climbed over a mile since leaving home.

"Is it going to be hard to breathe here since we'll be so high up?"

"It might be," his mom answered. "Before you and Nick were born, your dad and I took a trip out west, and it was tough to breathe at first—especially if you're hiking or running. Some people get headaches. But your body adapts, and it gets easier. Plus, drinking lots of water helps."

Jake searched around on the floor for his water bottle and gulped down as much as he could.

It was late, so all the T-shirts, ice cream, and taffy stores were closed when they drove through town. But it didn't take long before the buildings and lights of Estes Park disappeared. Soon a big wooden sign came into view. Built upon a rock foundation, it read: *Rocky Mountain National Park, Established 1915.*

In front of them, the road split into several lanes, each with a small entry station. It was late, and the booths were closed for the night. Jake was surprised when his dad continued driving past the station and into the park. "Wait, are we just going to go in without paying?"

"Grandpa bought our national parks pass online, and we have our campsite reservation, so we're allowed to drive through," his dad explained as they followed the signs to the campground.

Jake peered into the darkness, trying to make out the landscape. After a minute, he gave up and leaned his head against the window. Driving into his first National Park at night was not what he had imagined. He was in the mountains for the first time in his life and couldn't even see them. And, with the guard stations closed, he would have to wait until tomorrow to find out more about the cabin in the photograph.

"We're here." His dad turned the truck into a narrow drive. "Moraine Park Campground."

"Another park inside of a park?" Jake asked. "Wait, let me guess. Moraine Park is another big valley in the middle of the mountains."

"You got it. Now, let's find our site. It's C 240."

Locating the site, Mr. Evans backed the camper into the designated spot and turned off the truck.

When Jake stepped out, he immediately knew that he was in a whole new world. The crackle of campfires mingled with the distant voices of campers who had yet to turn in for the night. Jake took in a deep breath, and the cool mountain air stung the insides of his nose and lungs. The butterscotch smell of pine sap and the scent of sagebrush mixed with smoke from the fires. Their light cast a soft, orange glow upon nearby pine boughs.

He walked over to the side of the camper, unlocked a panel, and took out two sets of tire chocks. He put the heavy rubber triangles on both sides of each of the camper's tires. This would keep it from rolling away when they detached it from the truck's towing hitch.

"What's next, Dad?" Jake put his hands on his hips and yawned.

"You can get in the camper, pull your bed out, and get some sleep. We'll sort out anything else that needs to be done in the morning."

Jake grabbed the scrapbook and his overnight bag from the backseat of the truck and got settled in the camper. After he was in bed, he slid open the window beside him. In the distance, he could hear the water of a stream, then the hoot of a great-horned owl. He fell asleep dreaming of the places he would explore in the morning.

CHAPTER 4

1880

The boy lay completely still in the rafters, breathing through his nose and trying not to move. The makeshift loft was littered with burlap sacks, bundles of twine, and a nearly empty bottle of something caramel-colored. From his perch, he could hear the men's muffled voices and see the top of the shed's door. The pink light of dusk began to fade.

All grew quiet as the deep blues of night crept over the ranch. Silence. Then footsteps. A clinking of spurs getting closer. The sound of the door's metal latch.

He watched the door swing open. There was a pause. Then he heard the man swear.

"The kid escaped!"

His plan was working.

Next came the sounds of men and horses, whistles,

and the ranch boss yelling, "Hee-ya!" Hoofbeats tore off into the distance.

The boy stayed put, waiting for twilight to become darkness. When it came, he climbed down from the rafters and slipped out the door into the night. Drawn by his curiosity, he headed back to the creek. He had something to dig out of the ground.

He searched for his pack and found it where he had stashed it in the rocks along the creek. The moon was up now, nearly full and illuminating the mountain peaks in the west. He made his way to the marker: two fallen aspen trees, one set across the other. This was where the boss, the man in the leather cowboy hat, had buried it.

The boy kneeled at the spot and clawed at the ground until his fingers scraped across something made of cloth. He pulled a velvet bag from the dirt and dusted it off. He had to know what was inside. What slid out of the bag was about the size of his hand, triangular and rounded. A layer of dirt covered much of its surface. At first, he thought it was a rock. Then part of it glinted in the moonlight. *Silver! That's why it feels so heavy.*

He hesitated. Before this moment, he was just an intruder, some kid who'd wandered into the wrong place at the wrong time. If he pushed the bag back into the earth, they might forget about him. If he put it into his pack, he was certain to be hunted. And he didn't take things that weren't his. But he had heard about this in town. A local woman had found a store of Indian relics, ancient things, in a pottery container hidden near the Old Ute Trail. People had been talking because someone had stolen one of the more valuable objects from her home. The rumor was that it was made of silver.

A sound in the distance broke the quiet of the night. Dogs. They had probably found his trail.

He had just seconds to decide.

He put the object back in its velvet pouch. Then he slipped the bag into his pack and melted into the darkness of the forest.

CHAPTER 5

MORAINE PARK

J ake woke before his parents. In fact, he was up and moving before anyone in the campground. He changed out of his PJs, grabbed his backpack, and tiptoed to the door, trying not to wake his parents. Stepping out the door, he was surprised by how cold it still was. He could see his breath. Jake slipped back into the camper, found his coat, and once again, made his way outside.

As he walked to the back of the campsite, everything he had hoped to see came into view. He couldn't believe his eyes. The tops of the mountains, still covered in snow, were lit by the dawn with pinks and blues. Below them were more mountains, covered in the deep greens of the forest. His eyes scanned across thousands of places he was yearning to explore. Just below the campground, a broad meadow stretched out before him.

He left the campsite and meandered down the hillside and into the meadow. He felt invited, drawn into the immense space by its beauty and by the sounds of water. The soft rushing sound grew louder with each step. A gray fog rose from the winding course of a stream, lit by the faint red light of dawn. He wandered down to the stream bank. Trout swam in its waters, and alongside the muddy banks, he spotted the immense tracks of some animal who must have come down in the night for a drink. Jake found a big rock, sat down, and took it all in.

Moraine Park

Something about this place was familiar. But that didn't make sense. Jake had never even been to Colorado, not to mention Rocky Mountain National Park.

As the sun continued to rise, birdsong filled the air. Further into the meadow, what he first thought were rocks or dark tufts of grass began moving. Elk. He scanned the field again. Female elk with baby calves ambled down to the stream. There were a few big bull elk like they had seen last night. A little bird flew right over Jake's shoulder, landed on a rock in front of him, and began bobbing up and down. Then it did something unexpected and dove beneath the water.

"Amazing, isn't it?"

Jake jumped at the sound of an unfamiliar voice and turned to look behind him to see a park ranger.

She was about his brother's age, and long blonde braids framed her face. Jake thought she was pretty. At the same time, he wondered if maybe he was in trouble. Perhaps he had missed a sign, and this place was off-limits.

"Am I not supposed to be here?" he asked and started to get up.

"You're just fine." The ranger pointed to the water. "That little bird is called a dipper. They are funny little things. They're the only songbirds in North America that will dive completely underwater. Did you notice how he bobs up and down?"

Jake relaxed, realizing that he wasn't in trouble. "I did. They look kind of silly. None of our birds back home do that."

"That's how they got their name: because they dip up and down like that when they walk."

Just then, the dipper popped to the surface of the water and began walking and bobbing along the rocks in the shallow part of the creek.

"My name is Jake." He stood up and offered the ranger his hand.

The young woman took it. "Ranger Musgrave, but you can call me Ellie."

When she said "Ranger," a thought popped into his head. She might be able to identify the cabin in the photograph.

"Um, Ellie, I wonder if you could help me with something?"

"Sure thing." Ellie tapped on her ranger badge and added, "That's part of my job. The ranger motto is '*Integrity, Honor, Service*'."

"Well, I have this old photograph that my grandpa took a long time ago. It's supposed to be something here in the park, and I'm trying to figure out where it is."

"Do you have the picture with you? I'd love to take a look at it."

Jake looked up the hill back at the campground. Ellie

turned around to follow his eyes. "I bet you left it back at camp."

"Yep. It's in the camper, and my parents are asleep."

"I tell you what," she replied, "I'm working at the Beaver Meadows Visitor Center today. What if you drop by with that photo, and we can have a look at it?"

"Sounds good. Thank you, Ellie."

"This is my first summer working here. But if I can't figure it out, there are rangers at the visitor center who I'm sure could help you."

"Okay, I'll see you later today."

Ranger Ellie gave Jake a nod, smiled, and turned to walk back across the meadow toward her white truck.

After his parents awoke and had breakfast, they got in the truck and drove up to the visitor's center. Jake stood outside its doors with a daypack slung over his shoulder.

"Do you know how to get back to the campground from here?" Mr. Evans asked.

"I've got the park map." Jake unfolded the map and pointed to their location. "We're here at the Beaver

Meadows Visitor Center. And we're staying at the Moraine Park Campground, right?"

"Correct."

"So, I can take this trail–" Jake ran his finger along a trail just south of the visitor center– "and it will lead back into Moraine Park."

"Sounds like a good plan. We'll see you around lunchtime."

Jake felt independent and proud that his parents trusted him with this short adventure. He had prepared for the hike by loading his daypack with water, some trail mix, and a journal. Stepping into the visitor center, he scanned the room for anyone wearing a green hat and uniform.

His eyes were drawn to the center of the large, open room. A few people were gathered around what looked like a huge map. But instead of being flat, this map had texture. The mountains rose from its surface. Rivers, painted in blue, snaked through the miniature landscape.

Jake walked around its wooden case, seeing what Rocky Mountain National Park would really look like from this bird's-eye view. There were buttons along the sides of the case. He pushed the one that read *Long's Peak,* and a small, red light atop the highest mountain lit up. When he pressed another button labeled *Alpine Visitor Center*, it caused another red light, high in the northern mountains, to shine.

Wow, he thought to himself, *they have a visitor center all the way up there?* After a moment more at the huge map, Jake returned to his search for Ellie.

He walked to the information desk and peeked through the office door, where he thought he had caught a glimpse of a ranger with blonde, braided hair.

"Can I help you?" asked a ranger who was so tall that he made his own hat look small.

Jake looked up. "I'm trying to find Ranger..." He tried to remember her last name,"...Ranger Graves?" he asked, certain that he had the name wrong.

The tall ranger thought for a minute. "Do you mean Ranger Musgrave?"

"Yes, that's it," Jake replied.

"She's here. I'll go find her."

The ranger turned and went into the office. A moment later, Ellie came out.

"Hi, Jake," she said while walking up to the counter. "Did you bring the photo?"

Jake was impressed that she'd remembered his name. It made him feel important.

"I did." He handed her the photograph.

"Wow, it looks a little different, but I know exactly where this is—and it's not very far from here."

"No way!" Having walked around the giant map of the park, he understood just how big the park was. He expected the cabin would be miles away, hidden deep in the woods.

"This cabin now serves as our backcountry office. It's where you go to plan backpacking trips into the heart of the park," she explained. "Do you have a map?"

"I have this one." Jake pulled the folded visitor guide out of his back pocket. He opened it onto the counter and flipped to the side with the map of the park.

"We're here, right?" Jake said, pointing to the little black square marking the visitor center.

"Right," she replied. Ellie drew a pen out of her pocket. "Do you mind if I mark the location of the cabin on here?"

"Sure thing."

She put an X on the map just east of the visitor center. "If you go out those doors and turn right, you'll see the restrooms. Walk past the restrooms until you come to a trail. That trail will take you down to the cabin."

"Thanks, Ellie." Jake folded the map and put it back in his pocket.

She handed the picture back to him and leaned onto the counter. "Jake, I think you're going to need a better map."

"What do you mean?"

"Well, the map in your pocket is meant for driving around the park. It's the free one we give to every visitor.

But I can tell you're an explorer. So, you're going to need a *topographical* map. We call them 'topo' maps for short. I'll be right back."

She walked out from behind the counter and into the gift shop, pausing to talk with the woman at the cash register. She returned and unfolded a much larger map onto the counter across from Jake. As he studied it, Jake became overwhelmed by all of its markings. This was completely different from the map in his back pocket. This one showed over one hundred trails, and *every* creek and mountain was labeled with its name.

"It's really different, isn't it?" she asked.

"*Way* different," Jake replied.

"See these lines that look like fingerprints?" She pointed out the strange rings that covered the entire map.

"Yeah, what are those for?"

"These are called contour lines. They tell you how steep or gentle a slope is. On the ground, the space between each line is fifty feet."

Jake followed her finger as she slid it over to where it read *Ypsilon Mountain 13,514'*.

"This is one of the most beautiful mountains in the park. See how the lines get closer together here just to the west of the Spectacle Lakes?"

"That means it's super steep right there?"

"Correct. And when the lines are farther apart, like

right here–" Ellie ran her finger along the Ypsilon Lake Trail–"it means that it's a more gentle slope. You'll find that most hiking trails will follow the more gentle slopes."

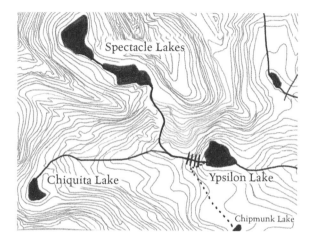

"Like this one over here?" Jake pointed to a place on the map that read, "Cow Creek Trail."

"Exactly. That trail starts off gently, but you'll also notice that the terrain becomes steep here at the end, by the waterfall."

"There's a waterfall back in there?" Jake wanted to hear more.

"Yes. See those the two blue dashes that run perpendicular to the creek?"

"That means there's a waterfall?"

"It does. But sometimes, it's just a cascade."

"What's the difference?"

"A cascade is where water tumbles over rocks, and a waterfall is when the water drops through the air."

"That makes sense," Jake said. "This is amazing! It's so much better than the other map."

"It's yours." She folded the map and handed it to him. "It's on me."

"Wow, thank you." He took the map and slid it into his backpack.

"How long are you and your family staying?" she asked.

"Counting today, we'll be here five full days."

"There's a lot to explore in that time. Have fun. And I hope you find what you're looking for at the cabin."

Jake thanked Ellie for all her help. It was time to hike to the cabin and figure out what his grandfather had in store for him.

CHAPTER 6

AT THE OLD CABIN

Jake found the trail precisely where Ranger Ellie had described it. Its course passed under the shade of tall ponderosa pines and curved downhill to a small parking lot and an old cabin.

He pulled out the photograph. It was a perfect match, except that now the building had a sign on the side that read *Backcountry Permits.* He stepped inside. On his right was a big stone fireplace. Maps and old photographs decorated the wood-planked walls. One of the signs showed the drawing of a bear and read: *Enjoy them at a distance.* The rest of the cabin contained a long counter and an office area behind the counter where several rangers worked.

Jake walked up to the counter, and a man about his dad's age looked up from his computer.

"If you're here to get a backcountry permit, you'll need to come back with a parent."

"Oh, no. I just have a question."

The man took his eyes off the computer screen and looked at Jake. "Well then, hopefully, I can answer it."

"I'm looking for someone named Jasper. I was told I could find him here."

The man grinned, turned his head, and called back into the offices, "Jasper, you've got a visitor."

The ranger left as an older man, who Jake supposed was Jasper, approached. He appeared to be in his seventies, had a neatly trimmed white beard, and wore wire-rimmed glasses. After seeing Jake, he went to a calendar hanging on a nearby wall. He ran his finger along the current week, and tapped on May 28th. "You must be Jake Evans."

Before Jake could respond, the man went back to his office. The jingle of keys cut through the silence before the click of a lock and the sound of a drawer opening. Then the man returned with a package about the size of a shoebox and wrapped in brown paper. He set it on the counter and pushed it across to Jake. "You'll want to put that in your pack right quick."

Jasper's brow wrinkled with caution as his eyes shifted to the door like a hawk scanning a field from its perch.

Jake zipped the pack shut and asked, "How did you know my name?"

Jasper took his eyes from the door and looked at Jake. "The same reason you knew mine." He reached out and offered his hand to Jake. As they shook hands, he introduced himself formally. "I'm Jasper Carlson. Your grandfather said you'd be coming by here on May 28th or 29th."

"He did?"

"He sure did," Jasper replied. "I'm sorry to hear of his passing. He was a good man and a good friend."

"So, he left the package for me?"

"Well, kinda." Jasper's voice grew quieter. "It arrived here last week from New Mexico."

Jake's eyebrows narrowed in confusion. "Mr. Jasper, I'm sorry, but I don't understand. My grandpa passed away months ago."

"I can't say much, kid. It's not safe." Jasper glanced back at the door, and then spoke in a hushed voice. "I was friends with your grandfather—a whole group of us were. We had a club of sorts that met using our ham radio systems. Before your grandfather passed, he told me that you'd be coming here and that I was to give you a package from *The Keeper*."

"The Keeper?"

"We don't know *the Keeper* by his real name–just his radio handle: Mather." The old man's eyes darted around the room. "Kid, I wish I could tell you more, but it's just not safe to talk about it out in the open."

"Why not?" Jake asked.

Jasper didn't answer. He just smiled and put his hand out again. When Jake shook it, he realized that it was more than a goodbye. It felt like he had just made some kind of deal. Jake secured the backpack over his shoulders and began walking out the door.

"Jake," Jasper called him back.

Jake stopped at the threshold and turned around.

Jasper's serious eyes softened, and he smiled. "Jake, we trust you."

Outside the cabin, Jake pulled out his map and found the trail that led back to camp. It took all his willpower not to unzip his backpack, pull out the package and open it. Was Jasper just paranoid? Jake had seen older people go downhill and act strange. But aside from his vigilance, Jasper seemed normal enough.

Jake hiked until he spotted a secluded area on the hill above him concealed within a cluster of pine trees. He left the trail, and when he was sufficiently hidden within the woods, he sat down and pulled out the package.

On the top, he read:

Rocky Mountain National Park
Backcountry Office
Attn: Jasper Carlson
Mills Drive
Estes Park, Colorado 80517

The top left, where the return address would be, only read:

Mather
Gallina, New Mexico
87017

Mather had wrapped the box in thick brown paper, like a Christmas present. Jake was tearing at a seam when something went *snap* behind him in the forest. He froze, then slowly looked over his shoulder. Twenty yards away stood a doe and a spotted fawn. Jake was surprised by how fast his heart was beating, both in anticipation of what might be inside the package and with the fear that someone might be watching. The deer moved on and disappeared over the hill behind him.

Jake unwrapped the package to reveal a cardboard box secured with packing tape. He pulled off the tape and drew out a smaller wooden box. It was about as long and wide as a large cell phone and about five inches deep. The edges and corners were covered with worn leather strips that were secured to the box with brass button tacks. The wood was weathered, as it had seen many years. And it was nicked and scratched in places, like scars, each with their own story to tell. But the box showed the signs of care too. Someone had polished its surface with oil.

Inside the package and under a pile of Styrofoam packing peanuts, he found a piece of paper. He pulled it out and read it:

```
Burn the package and burn this note.
THEY know I have it, and it's no longer
safe with me. I'm number 23, which
makes you Keeper 24. Here are the
instructions I received from 22:
You are its steward and protector,
charged to keep it hidden. Discover
what can be discovered and find the
next Keeper. All we've learned has
been entrusted to the Marmot.
```

Jake now understood that Mather had been the last *Keeper. But keeper of what? Who's the Marmot?* Jake wondered. *And who are "they"?*

He turned the box over, looking for some way to open it. He could tell by the seam that it had a lid, but there were no hinges, latch, or lock mechanism where a key might fit. He gently shook it, but it didn't make a sound. Whatever was inside had been packed such that it wouldn't move—and it was heavy—way heavier than he could have imagined by looking at its size. That's when it hit him. *Could it be gold?* In science class, he had learned that gold weighed almost three times as much as metals like iron and steel. The thought made Jake's chest buzz with excitement and his head spin with curiosity. There had to be some way to get into the box.

His thoughts were interrupted by a series of beeps. The sound felt out of place among the hushed woods, and he quickly reached into his backpack to silence the alarm he'd set on his watch. It was supposed to remind him when he needed to return to camp, but now it could also alert anyone nearby to his hiding spot among the trees. He needed to get going.

He put the box back into the package, stuck it in his backpack, and hurried out of the woods back down to the trail. As he hiked back to Moraine Park, his thoughts swirled: Gold, Keeper, Mather, *They*, Marmot. But he noticed his mind kept returning to one thing, something Jasper said: *We trust you.* Those words made Jake think this scavenger hunt was somehow more than just a game. And he hoped the next clue would help him make sense of it.

CHAPTER 7

1880

The boy had traveled by moonlight for at least three hours. He didn't own a watch, but he could tell it was near midnight by the moon's position in the sky. It was early June, and the chill of the night air caused him to shiver. He decided to risk a small fire.

He broke dead branches from a spruce tree and gathered dry moss from its higher branches. Taking a flint stick out of his pack, he scraped his knife against it, throwing sparks into the nest of moss until it ignited into a small orange flame.

When he was warm, the boy pulled a small notebook from his jacket pocket. A ticket fell from its pages onto the ground. It read: *Union Pacific Railway - Denver.* He picked the ticket up and placed it back into the journal, unwrapped the end of a small loaf of bread from a cloth, and ate his last bites of food. After writing some notes in the journal, he leaned back against a rock and shut his eyes.

A sound in the distance jolted him awake. The fire was low. He listened. A series of sharp barks cut through the night.

He hurried to extinguish the fire, swung his pack over his shoulder, and ran downhill. Now, he could hear the voices of men. Racing through the forest, he found a creek and ran through it, hoping to throw the dogs off his scent. He stumbled over the slick, round rocks. The creek was a smart move, but it slowed his pace, and soon his boots were soaked through with water. To his right lay a broad and open glade. It was too exposed. He ran to the left, only to find that he was at the rim of a deep ravine. The voices and barks grew louder. He could hear the splash of water and the snap of branches.

With nowhere else to go, he scrambled down the steep side of the gully by holding onto the trunks of a few aspen trees. Finding a narrow shelf of rock, he edged out onto it, leaning against the face of the cliff and tucking himself into the shadows.

Seconds later, the dogs arrived at the top of the ravine, their barks echoing off its rock walls. Twenty feet above him, hooves tore at the ground, and a horse blew a long sigh through its nostrils. The boy's legs shook from exhaustion, fear, and the cold, but he tried to stay still. He heard a man's voice: "His trail stops here. Chances are he fell. We'll check the canyon in the morning to see if there's a body."

The men turned their horses around and whistled for the dogs to follow. After waiting for the sounds to fade into the forest, the boy inched his way back to the steep side of the ravine and made his way back to the rim. When he'd left Pennsylvania three weeks ago, it had not been his plan to be running from cowboys.

He gazed into the starry western sky, where the snow-capped mountains gleamed an icy blue in the moonlight. Though he had already been locked up, chased down, and had nearly plunged to his death, this place called to him. The wildness of it felt like home—something he had never experienced before.

Below him and far beyond the ravine, he spied little orange lights. He squinted, studying the spot until he realized they were lanterns being lit in the windows of a house. Smoke curled out its chimney. He continued surveying what appeared to be another ranch. There were fences and small barns, and he could now make out the dark shape of cattle gathered near a copse of trees behind the house. The place looked like a haven in the wilderness.

Perhaps they needed help. Maybe he could work for

food and a bed. Then again, they might hand him over to the men who were hunting him. Cold and weary, the boy decided to take the chance.

CHAPTER 8

WES

It was just past noon, and Jake was getting hungry. Soon he reached the ridge above the meadows of Moraine Park where he could look down to the campground road. As he got closer to camp, the smell of food on the grill caught his attention.

His mom stepped out of the camper. Seeing him, she called out, "Perfect timing, Jake. Your dad is grilling lunch. It'll be ready in five minutes. Uncle Brian and Aunt Judy should be here in an hour or two, and the Catalina's called and said they would be here later this afternoon."

"Did you find the cabin?" his dad asked.

"I did." Jake walked over to see what his dad was cooking for lunch. "It's where you go to get permits to camp in the park. While I was there, I met one of grandpa's old friends."

"That's incredible. But it makes sense. Your grandpa may have been the friendliest person on planet earth." His dad brushed more barbeque sauce onto the chicken. "Did he give you your next clue?"

"I think so. It's an old box with something heavy in it, but I can't figure out how to open it."

"Your mom and I are always willing to help."

At his dad's offer, Jake felt his body become tense. "I kinda want to do this on my own."

"Well, your cousin will be here soon," his mom said. "I'm sure Wes will be excited to help you with the scavenger hunt."

"Mom, I told you guys yesterday that I want to do this by myself." Jake's face flushed with frustration. "Please. Just don't tell Wes...or Amber, or their parents, or *anybody*."

His parents appeared a little surprised by the force of his response. Things were quiet for a moment, then his mom walked closer and put her hand on his shoulder. "I understand. If I were in your shoes, I'd want to figure things out for myself too."

His dad nodded in agreement and flipped the chicken on the grill. The sauce dripped onto the flames and sizzled.

"Do you guys promise?"

Jake's mom crossed her heart, and his dad held out his pinky.

"You guys are so weird," Jake said as he walked up to his dad to take his pinky promise.

They were interrupted by the throaty sound of a diesel engine. An RV with a jeep in tow pulled alongside their campsite, and someone inside rolled down the window. The man in the driver's seat had a thick red beard. He wore a trucker's hat and a pair of gold-lens sunglasses. "Hey, sister!" he called out.

"Brian! Judy! You guys are early!" Jake's mom exclaimed, almost jumping out of her shoes.

"Where should we park?" Uncle Brian asked.

"Take the site to the east." Mr. Evans pointed out the spot with the metal spatula. "That way, your RV will create more shade for all of us."

"Smart thinking, Evans." Uncle Brian tapped his forehead with his finger, then pointed at Jake's dad and smiled.

As much as Jake was not excited about having company, he really liked his uncle. He was funny and knew a lot about the outdoors.

A few moments later, the RV engine went silent, and the side door flew open. Out came a kid who looked like he'd just woken from a nap. Wes's red hair spiraled out into an afro, with one side flattened from how he'd slept. Dark brown freckles covered his light brown skin. He wore a shirt that read: *Built for the Wild*. A hatchet was attached to his belt, and a compass hung around his neck.

Wes walked quickly toward Jake like he was going to hug him. But he stopped short. After an awkward second, he put out his hand. "Hey, Jake!"

"Hey, Wes. Glad you guys made it." Jake shook Wes's hand.

Jake wanted to say, "What's with the hatchet and the compass?" but he knew that would be rude.

"You ready to go hiking?" Wes asked.

"Well, we were just about to eat some lunch." Jake motioned toward the food on the grill. "We could throw another burger on for you."

Wes's shoulders slumped in disappointment, but the prospect of food quickly revived his spirits.

Mrs. Evans walked over and gave her nephew a hug. "Wes, you're going into seventh grade next year, right?"

"Sure am. I might even take some advanced classes for high school credit."

"That's exciting." She handed Wes a paper plate.

"Yeah, but it would mean more homework. I'm not looking forward to that."

Aunt Judy and Uncle Brian walked over. Jake had always been awed by the presence of his aunt. She had been a national champion pole-vaulter at the college where she had met Uncle Brian. When Jake was younger, he noticed how people stared at them, like they were trying to figure out a puzzle. They saw Aunt Judy's dark brown skin and her husband's chalky-white, freckled face. Her hair was dark, and his was a blaze of red. They noticed how Judy was much taller than her husband. And then there was their son, who broke all their categories. But to Jake, all three of them were athletic and confident and fun.

Uncle Brian wrapped Jake up in a hug that felt like being squeezed by a grizzly bear. He set Jake down and put his hand on Jake's shoulder. "Jake, I think you've grown a good six inches since we saw you last."

Jake nodded and smiled.

"Wesley, you should ask your cousin if he could help with that new tent of yours."

"Oh, yeah." Wes ran back into the RV and returned with a blue cloth bag. "Mom and Dad got me this new tent for the trip. It's a 3-man, so it will fit the both of us if you want to sleep over. Could you help me put it up?"

"Sure. Where do you want to put it?"

"There's a tent pad on the other side of the RV." Wes nodded in the direction, and Jake followed.

As the boys set up the tent and ate lunch, Jake's eyes darted to the camper where he had left his backpack that contained the mysterious box. He had become distracted by Wes's arrival and left it sitting on his bunk. Along the campground road, a man walked his black labrador retriever. Other campers were taking down their tents and packing up their gear. Jake felt uneasy, like he was being watched. He needed a few minutes alone to conceal the box and study the scrapbook for the next clue.

There was one good hiding place in the camper. At the table were two bench seats. Both were hinged at the back and opened to reveal storage compartments. One of these belonged to Jake, the other to his parents. Jake had hidden the scrapbook at the bottom of his, under a blanket, his backpack, a couple of jackets, some hats, and a pair of gloves. Moving these things out of the way, Jake hid the box Jasper had given him at the bottom and covered it up. He pulled the scrapbook out of its hiding place, closed the bench, and sat down at the table.

He opened the book and found the space for the picture of the cabin. As Jake began to slide the photograph back into its mounts, he saw a series of very faint dots and dashes written on the page. Jake took out a pencil and copied the characters onto a scrap of notebook paper.

• — —   •   •—•   •—   •—••   —••

•—•   — — —   — — —   —   •••

Just then, someone rapped on the door. Jake grabbed a blanket and threw it over the scrapbook. But as the blanket fell, it blew the scrap of paper onto the floor.

"Come in," Jake called.

Wes opened the door. "Hey...Jake...guess what?" he said, trying to catch his breath.

"You've just been chased by a bear, and that's why you're so out of breath?"

"No, don't be silly. I just ran here from our campsite."

"But it's, like, twenty feet away."

"It's the altitude...It's hard to breathe here. Anyway, my parents and your parents said we..." Wes took in a few more deep breaths. "...they said we could pick the hike for tomorrow!"

"Cool," Jake replied, his mind still distracted by the strange symbols.

Wes picked something up off the floor. "Whoa! Did you write this?"

Jake was unsure how to respond. He hesitated and thought for a moment. "Yeah, just for fun."

Wes continued examining the paper. "I didn't know you understood morse code!"

Morse code. That was it. That's why it felt familiar. When Jake was ten, his parents had given him a set of walkie-talkies for Christmas, and they'd each had a sticker on them with morse code symbols and their matching letters of the alphabet.

"Why are you doing morse code, Jake?"

Jake tried to sidestep the question by asking another. "Do you understand it?"

"I sure do. Do you mind if I decode it?"

"Um, yeah, go for it."

Wes plopped down at the table and asked for the pencil. He began writing out the message, letter by letter, saying each letter out loud as he wrote. "E, M, E, R... My friend Chase and I learned morse code last year," Wes continued. "That way, we could communicate during class without passing notes...A...L...D...R...We would tap our pencils and send messages. But then we got in trouble for all the tapping...O...O...T...S."

The boys looked down at the completed message.

EMERALDROOTS

"I think it's two words." Wes drew a line between the D and the R.

"Emerald Roots?" Jake said in a puzzled voice.

"Not sure why you're confused, Jake. You wrote the message."

Jake tried to change the subject. "So, we get to pick the hike for tomorrow, right?"

"We do." Wes stood up from the table and pushed the paper over to Jake. "I was thinking we could go to this waterfall that the guy at the next campsite told us about. It's not a long hike, and there are all kinds of other places we can go from there. But I hear there is snow, so we might need snowshoes."

"There's snow?" Jake was bewildered. "But it's almost June."

"The trail starts at Bear Lake, and there's still a bunch of snow up there. That's what the guy told my dad." Wes paused as a new thought hit him. "Hey, did you write *emerald* because you want to go to that lake? Because we could go there too."

"What do you mean?"

"I mean that there is a lake called Emerald Lake here. Isn't that why you wrote 'emerald' in your code?"

"That's it!" Jake's voice rose with his excitement. Wes had figured out at least the first half of the message. "Is that near the waterfall you want to see?"

"I'm not sure." Wes reached back and began pulling something out of his back pocket. "I've got this map. They gave it to us at the park entrance. But it's not all that helpful. I wish we had a good map."

Jake reached into his backpack and pulled out the map Ranger Ellie had given him. "You mean a map like this?"

"That's perfect!"

Seeing the map seemed to have jogged Wes's memory. "Jake, I totally forgot something else. My dad said our parents want to talk to us about something at dinner tonight."

"About what?"

"No clue. I tried to get it out of Dad, but he wouldn't tell me."

The camper door opened. It was Jake's mom. "Boys, the Catalinas are here. Come on out to greet them."

CHAPTER 9

MISSION

J ake opened the door to see a woman his mom's age walking toward them along the campground road. She had a contagious smile and dark brown hair pulled back into a ponytail. Walking beside her was a girl who looked like an almost exact copy of her mom. Both wore shorts, t-shirts, hiking socks, and boots. Jake's mom ran to greet them.

"Jacqueline, it's so good to see you!" She gave Mrs. Catalina a hug. "And, Amber, you've grown so much since our last visit. You look so much like your mom."

"Thanks, Mrs. Evans." Amber gave a nervous smile and raked her hand through her hair.

This was not the Amber who Jake remembered from five years ago when the Catalinas had visited their home in Ohio. The first thing he noticed was that she was nearly as tall as him. Jake straightened up. He had grown so much in the last year that his parents would often say things like, "You're slumping again," or "Don't slouch." He was always forgetting. But in this moment, he remembered.

Amber had long golden-brown hair with a bright purple streak that fell across the left side of her face. Her skin was dark, like her parents.

"Jake and Wes, come over here." Mrs. Evans motioned for the boys to join them.

They walked up, and the introductions began. Wes was obviously thrilled to meet new people and became very talkative. Jake got very quiet, nervously rubbing the pocket of his hiking pants with one of his hands. He didn't want to admit that he was embarrassed by his cousin's excitement. But if he kept standing there still as a tree, not saying a word, he would appear impolite and awkward. So, he decided to ask Amber a question. "How was your trip here?"

Amber shrugged. "There was a lot of desert between California and Colorado, so kinda boring. It's nice to see trees again."

"Where is Luis?" Mrs. Evans asked.

"He's checking in with the campground attendant." Mrs. Catalina pointed back toward the campground entrance. "We were so excited to see you guys that we just couldn't wait."

Mrs. Catalina's accent sounded very different from her daughter's. She and her husband were from Argentina, where Amber had been born. But Amber had lived twelve of her thirteen years in northern California.

"Jake and Wes, when Mr. Catalina pulls up, could you help him get them settled in?" Mrs. Evans asked.

"Sure thing," both boys said at the same time.

A few minutes later, Luis Catalina arrived, backed the camper into the site beside them, and got out to greet everyone. He shook Jake's hand. "Jake, you're two feet taller than I remember you. And you must be Wesley." He extended his hand to Wes.

"Yes, sir. You can call me Wes."

"And you boys can both call me Luis. None of that 'sir' stuff needed here."

Luis Catalina had dark eyebrows, a nose that looked like it was from a Roman sculpture, and a thin, dark beard and mustache. Jake didn't know much about the Catalinas, but he did remember that Mr. Catalina had a job doing top-secret stuff for a company that worked for the government—something to do with missiles. Jake had always thought that was cool.

While helping Amber put up her hammock, Jake noticed that Uncle Brian was talking with her parents about something. His uncle glanced over at them. Amber's parents did the same.

"I bet they're talking about tonight," Wes said.

"What about tonight?" Amber asked.

Wes tightened the nylon strap around the tree trunk to secure the hammock. "After dinner, there's something they want to talk with us about."

Amber looked at Wes and Jake. "You guys have any idea what it is?"

Wes shrugged his shoulders. "No clue."

That evening, the dads put two picnic tables next to one another so that the three families could eat dinner together. The Catalina family made the meal, an Argentine barbeque called *asado*, skewers of steak, sausage, pork, and roasted potatoes. Amber brought over plates of hot sweetbread, then came back with dishes of chimichurri sauce. Jake looked across the table at Wes, who was taking in the feast before them. He looked up at Jake. "I think I'm in heaven."

"Speaking of heaven–" Mr. Catalina folded his hands– "let's give thanks for our food."

The families held hands and bowed their heads as Mr. Catalina prayed a blessing in Spanish. When he was finished, he clapped and smiled at the boys. *"Vamos a comer!* Let's eat!"

After dinner, Jake and Wes were assigned dish duty. When they were almost finished, Uncle Brian stepped out of his RV carrying a pack of chocolate bars, a box of graham crackers, and a big bag of marshmallows. "Who's ready for some s'mores?" he called out.

The boys furiously dried the last of the dishes and rushed over to where Uncle Brian was handing out the roasting sticks. Soon the scents of toasted marshmallows and melted chocolate surrounded the campfire. Jake watched Amber hold her marshmallow close to the coals until it ignited. She pulled it from the fire, patiently let it burn for a few seconds, and then blew out the flame.

"Perfect," she whispered to herself, satisfied with its caramel brown color.

Everyone was in various stages of roasting and eating their dessert when Uncle Brian cleared his throat. "We have a challenge for you kids."

This got Jake's, Amber's, and Wes's attention.

"The parents got together this afternoon." Uncle Brian leaned forward in the firelight. "And we were talking about all the amazing places we'll be visiting over these next two months and how you three are now old enough to want to do some things on your own. So, we decided that we want to allow you to go hiking and exploring without us following you around all the time. And—we want you to be safe."

Jake, Amber, and Wes looked at each other, amazed their parents would allow them to adventure out on their own. The parks they'd visit were untamed and wild places, full of beauty–and sometimes dangers.

"This is a once-in-a-lifetime opportunity for you," Uncle Brian continued, "to master stuff you could never learn in school, like how to predict the weather and read maps, what gear and food to pack, and all kinds of things about plants and wildlife."

"Dad," Wes said. "What did you mean by it being a challenge?"

"We want to give you some group assignments."

The three kids let out a collective groan. This was now starting to sound like a bad school project.

Uncle Brian laughed. "Okay, think of these as *missions* instead."

"That sounds way better," Jake replied. All three kids were now leaning in, interested in what Uncle Brian would say next.

"We want you three to plan your own adventures, and

by 'plan,' I mean you will need to write out your itinerary each time and give us a clear ETA. That's your *estimated time of arrival* back at the campground or the trailhead where we'll pick you up."

Mr. Evans sat down in a camp chair next to Uncle Brian. "We want to see that you're really thinking things through. You'll need to know the weather forecast, pack the best gear, clothes, and food—that kind of thing. Each trip—I'm sorry, *mission*—will be an opportunity for you three to build trust with the six of us parents."

Uncle Brian looked at each of the kids. "The more trust you build with us, and the more skills and knowledge you gain on your missions, the more we'll feel confident allowing you to explore on your own."

Jake looked over to see Amber, who was lit by the fire-light, raising her hand.

"Yes, Amber, you have a question?" Uncle Brian asked.

"Yeah, I was wondering about writing the itinerary. How do we do that?"

"It's going to be a list of places you plan to go and the trails you plan to take to get there. So, if something were to happen, we would know how to work with the rangers to find you. There are way too many stories about people who have died in the backcountry but would have survived if they'd just left an itinerary with a friend or family member." Jake looked at his mom. "Sounds like a good reason to bring a cell phone."

She gave him a mean stare that turned into a subtle smile.

Uncle Brian began fishing something out of his jacket pocket. "Yes, we are going to send a cell phone with you kids. But remember, they rarely work out here in the parks. You would have to go to a high spot to get reception— even then, you might not be able to get a signal. That's why we're also giving you this." He walked around the fire and put a black-and-orange device into Amber's hand. It was about the size of a cell phone and square.

She turned it over in her hand. "What is it?"

"It's an emergency beacon. If you were to get lost, or if something were to go wrong, you could push that button, and it would send us a text with your location. It would also alert the local search-and-rescue teams."

Wes looked over at the device, then to his dad. "How can it know our location and send a text if there's no cell reception?"

"It uses satellites instead of cell towers to communicate."

"Cool," Wes said as Amber passed the beacon to him.

"Okay–" Uncle Brian clapped his hands– "pop quiz."

"Dad, you've got to stop using school language."

"Whoops." Uncle Brian clapped his hand over his

mouth. "I promise. Instead, let's pretend you're on a game show. If you three can answer *this* question, then you'll win that last chocolate bar."

The kids leaned in to hear the question. Uncle Brian paused a few seconds for dramatic effect. Something in the campfire snapped, and a spark flew toward Jake and landed on the ground in front of him. He quickly stamped it into the dirt with his boot.

"What are the top three ways people die out in the wilderness?"

Jake, Amber, and Wes started discussing their answers. After a couple of minutes, they all nodded in agreement. Jake snapped his fingers. "Okay, I think we've got it: falling off cliffs and stuff, getting struck by lightning, and getting attacked by wild animals."

"Good answers. But only one is in the top three."

The kids regrouped and thought about it some more.

Wes offered the next answer. "Maybe just getting lost and starving or something?"

Amber pursed her lips in frustration. She obviously didn't like being wrong. "Maybe it has something to do with not bringing a first-aid kit. Let's think, what in a first-aid kit could save your life?"

Wes suddenly got excited. "Oh, oh, one of those, um, those snakebite kits! Dad, how about getting bit by a snake?"

"It can happen, but it's not in the top three." Uncle Brian held up three fingers and shook his head. "But you're on the right track. Keep thinking through your first-aid kit and your Ten Essentials."

"Ten Essentials?" Jake asked.

By this time, the kids had noticed that the parents were discussing the question, too. Other than Uncle Brian, it appeared that none of them knew the answers.

"The Ten Essentials are the things that you always need to carry in your backpack," Wes said. "I don't remember all of them, but it's stuff like a knife, water, matches, extra clothes..."

"I've got it!" Amber looked at both of the boys. "You need matches for fire and extra clothes to stay warm. You know how a lot of first-aid kits have that silver plastic emergency blanket thing? All those things are for keeping warm."

"Yes, that's got to be one of them!" Jake gave Amber a fist bump. "Uncle Brian, is one of the top three *freezing to death*?"

"Bingo!" He pointed at Amber to give her the credit. "Well done. Number three on the list is hypothermia— getting so cold that your body shuts down, and you die. You've got number one, which is dying from a fall. All you need is to guess number two."

"Could the Ten Essentials help us figure this one out?" Amber asked.

"Nope, not really. Instead, think about what you might encounter on a hike."

"We've already said getting attacked by an animal and snakes..." Wes rubbed his chin and stared into the fire. "So it can't be any of those."

"How about an avalanche?" Jake offered.

"You're close, but that's not in the top three." Uncle Brian sat back in his camp chair and put his hands behind his head.

Jake decided to see if he could get more information out of his uncle. "Why is it close? Do you mean getting crushed by a rockslide or something?"

"Just think about it a bit more. You'll get it."

Amber began thinking out loud. "If it's number two on the list, then it's got to be something people see a lot when they are out in the parks."

"Yes, and it's something they underestimate," Uncle Brian added.

"Water!" Wes called out. "I bet it's water."

"Yes, that's it!" Amber looked at Uncle Brian. "It's drowning in a river or a lake or something."

"Correct!" Uncle Brian tossed the chocolate bar over the fire to the kids. Amber caught it and began splitting it with the two boys.

"You now know the top three: falling, drowning, and hypothermia. I want you to keep those hazards in mind when you create your itineraries. You can avoid all three of them if you plan things out and make good decisions."

"Uncle Brian brought a lot of gear that you guys can use," Jake's dad explained. "And guidebooks, too. From his years in the Army and living in Idaho, he knows a lot about survival, first aid, and how to travel in the mountains. So, he's going to be a great person to talk to when you're planning."

"Can we go on our first hike tomorrow?" Amber asked. "By ourselves?"

"Yes, you can," Uncle Brian answered. "We'll drive up to the Bear Lake trailhead tomorrow after breakfast. You three should go put your plan together."

That night, Jake, Amber, and Wes sat at the booth in the camper planning their trip. With the map spread out before them, they began writing out their itinerary. They would start at Bear Lake and hike to Alberta Falls, the waterfall Wes had mentioned. Then, Jake suggested, they could hike in a loop, one that would take them to the trail for Emerald Lake.

"See, our trail would make a big loop, with a short side trail to this lake." Jake pointed to Lake Haiyaha on the map. "Then we could get back on the loop and hike up to this second side trail for Emerald Lake."

"That extra trail to Emerald Lake is a lot longer than the one that goes to Lake Haiyaha." Wes pointed it out on the map.

"Yeah, it's about half a mile from the loop trail to Emerald Lake," Jake replied. "But I think we can do it."

"First, we should total up all the miles," Amber said.

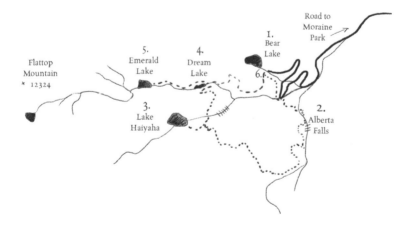

Jake began writing down the numbers from the map. "The loop is about four-and-a-half miles. And the side hikes to the lakes add about one and a half miles. So, the whole thing would be six miles."

"Okay, so how do we figure out how long it's going to take to go six miles?" Amber asked.

"Oh, I totally know this one." Wes shot out of his seat. "I mean, I know where to find out. I'll be right back." Wes ran out the door and soon returned with a book titled *Trekking and Land Navigation.* "Okay, it says here, most people hike about two miles per hour on flat trails. It takes longer going uphill and is a bit faster when you hike downhill."

"That's it?" Jake put his elbows on the table and stared at the map. "Two miles an hour seems super slow."

"That's what it says." Wes set the open book on the table in front of Jake.

Amber held up a finger and paused them for a second. "We should also plan time to take some breaks and pictures and stuff."

"Oh, right." Jake picked up the pencil again. "So, if it takes three hours for us to travel six miles, how much time should we add to the total?"

"I'm guessing about an hour," Amber offered.

"Okay, so that means if we leave at nine o'clock–" Jake began writing on their itinerary– "we should get back to meet Uncle Brian at the parking lot at one o'clock."

They finished their evening by packing their daypacks.

Then, after saying their goodnights, they each returned to their families and got ready for bed.

Jake lay in his loft. He could hear the hushed voices of their parents outside, still around the fire. He was tired, but he couldn't sleep. The excitement for tomorrow was pulsing through his veins. And he kept thinking about the clue, *Emerald Roots*, turning it over and over in his head. Eventually, the voices outside slowly faded, his thoughts wandered, and he drifted into sleep.

CHAPTER 10

1880

The light of dawn was waking the countryside as the boy descended into the meadow below the ravine. He could see a herd of elk grazing alongside the cattle behind the ranch buildings. A group of men gathered near what he assumed were their bunkhouses. After last night, his instinct was to turn and run. But to where? Back into the woods to hide and starve? He went to the front door of the main cabin and knocked.

He could hear footfalls on the floorboards inside. The door opened. A man, still with his fingers on the door handle, looked him in the eyes. He appeared to be about thirty years old and had a bushy mustache that covered his mouth, but no beard. His equally bushy eyebrows made him look stern and serious. The man turned from the open door and went back inside. As he walked away, he said, "I figured you might show up."

Fear overtook the boy. He was sure his heart was going to beat right out of his chest. But before he could turn and run, the man came back to the door with two metal cups full of coffee in one hand and a bowl of what looked like oatmeal in the other. "Have a seat there, young man." He gestured toward a set of chairs on the porch and handed the boy one of the metal cups and the bowl.

They both sat down. The boy took a sip of the hot drink and hoped the man didn't notice that his nervous hands were shaking.

"You must be the fella they came by here searching for last night." The man took a sip of coffee. "I'm Abner Sprague, owner of this ranch." He put out his hand. The boy shook it.

"Well, young man. I know we are out here in the wild country, but we still have manners. Are you going to introduce yourself?"

The boy hesitated. He could see the man knew he was tense. "Sorry," Abner said, "I should first explain that anyone causing trouble for Dunraven is a friend of mine. Don't worry. I'm not going to turn you over to 'em. You've got my word on that."

The boy's body relaxed, and he breathed a sigh of relief. "Thank you, Mr. Sprague. My name's Abe."

"Just Abe?"

"Yes, sir. I have no last name. My mother, she left me at an orphanage in Philadelphia shortly after I was born. All I came with was a scrap of paper telling them my first name."

"Well, Abe, these mountains are the right spot for finding yourself." Abner pointed out toward the snow-covered peaks that surrounded the valley. "I bet there's a name out there for you."

"Mr. Sprague, is Dunraven the man who's been chasing me?"

"Yes. And no. That would be Theodore Whyte, the foreman of Dunraven's ranch. Dunraven is a gentleman. That means he hires folks like Ted Whyte to do his dirty work. Dunraven's men tear down fences, run cattle onto the property of homesteaders, that kind of thing."

"Why would they do that?"

"Well, Earl Dunraven—that's what they call him back in England, where he's from—has his mind on taking over this whole country here. Men like him can't enjoy a place unless they own every square inch of it."

Abe took a sip of his coffee. Abner whistled. A dog appeared on the porch and ran up to him to be scratched behind the ears. Abe reached over and petted the dog, which wagged its tail and raised its head for a quick nuzzle.

Abner smiled. "Well, Abe-with-no-last-name, I've got a proposition for you."

"Yes, sir?" Abe replied.

"If you help the boys build another bunkhouse, I think we can get ya a comfortable spot to sleep. If you help with the ranch, we can feed ya. And if you help me with an endeavor I've got, I think we might even find you a last name."

"I'd like that very much, Mr. Sprague. What's the project?"

"A trail." He pointed to the tallest mountain, its gray granite face lit by the pink morning light. "I've got it in my head to build a trail to the top of that mountain."

Abe stared at the mountain, unable to fathom how someone could get to the top.

"But there's just one small problem, Abe. First, we're going to have to return whatever it is Ted Whyte is saying you stole from Dunraven."

"Mr. Sprague, sir, I don't think I can do that."

"Explain yourself, son." Abner sat back in his chair to listen.

Abe told Abner about what he had learned in town, how a woman had discovered a stash of Indian treasures, and how one item—the most valuable one—had been stolen from her home."

"I only took it with the intention of returning it to its rightful owner."

Abner leaned back, took another sip of his coffee, and thought for a moment. "Well, Abe, you've gotten yourself into quite a pickle, and I reckon the only way out is to go further in."

A sense of dread gripped Abe's gut. "What do you mean, sir?"

"You're not going to like this, but I think we need to have a friendly conversation with Dunraven."

CHAPTER 11

EMERALD LAKE

The next morning, Jake, Wes, and Amber reviewed their itinerary with Uncle Brian. He showed them how to strap on their snowshoes and checked their gear.

"You three look like you're ready to go," he said. "Get something hearty to eat, and then we'll head out in thirty minutes."

After breakfast, they said goodbye to the rest of their parents and piled into Uncle Brian's jeep. The road turned and twisted its way through the forest up the mountainside to Bear Lake, where a long parking lot was already filling with cars. The kids got out, reviewed their route on the map one more time, then said goodbye to Uncle Brian.

"I'll meet you at the ranger station beside the lake at 1 o'clock."

"See you then, Dad," Wes yelled as they ran across the parking lot toward the lake.

The view at Bear Lake took them by surprise. The snow-capped mountains that had appeared so far away from their campsite now stood before them, their image reflected on the water's surface. Chipmunks ran about begging for food from the visitors, who were taking pictures of the landscape and posing for selfies to share with their friends.

Bear Lake

"We want to head south," said Amber. "That should be this way." She pointed to their left and began walking. The boys followed.

"How did you know which way was south?" Jake asked.

"It's pretty easy," she replied. "The mountains are in the west. So, if we are facing the mountains, then north is to our right, and south should be on our left."

Wes held out the compass that hung around his neck and checked it. "She's right."

Soon they encountered a sign pointing the way to Alberta Falls. The trail was busy with people, and because it was one of the more popular hikes, the snow had been packed down. In places, the snow gleamed like ice. Jake's boot found one of those spots. He lost his balance, falling backward into Wes, who caught him and stopped his fall.

"Be careful, Jake; you just about smashed me like a bug." Wes clapped Jake on the back and laughed.

"Thanks, Wes." Jake glanced at Amber to see if she had noticed, but she appeared to be looking at something up ahead. A group of people had stopped and were blocking the path.

"Why are they just standing there?" Wes asked.

"Because of *that*!" Amber said, stepping forward so she could see better.

A bighorn sheep stood right in the middle of the trail. Several more were coming down the steep hillside on their right. The sheep crossed to the other side and continued making their way down the mountain.

Wes pointed at them. "Did you know that bighorn sheep have rectangular pupils? It helps them see behind them."

"Wes, you know the most random facts," Amber replied.

"Those kinds of things just stick in my brain for some reason." Wes scrunched his mouth and shrugged. "I wish it was that easy to remember important stuff."

After the bighorns finished crossing the trail, the group of hikers began moving again. Soon, the sounds of water filled the kids' ears. They came around a bend, and the falls came into view. Swollen with the early summer snowmelt, the waters of Glacier Creek shot from a rock outcrop into the air, creating a stunning waterfall. They stood at the overlook, taking in its sight and sounds.

Alberta Falls

"How far have we gone?" Jake asked.

"It's about one and a half miles from Bear Lake to here at Alberta Falls," Amber replied.

"And that means we are about halfway to the next lake," Wes added. "What's its name again? All I remember is it sounds like the sound you make when you do a karate chop."

Jake and Amber laughed.

"It's Lake Haiyaha." Jake had already started moving down the trail. "Let's keep going."

Past the waterfall, there were fewer people. The trail was less packed down, but they could still travel without their snowshoes. Though the sky was blue, light snow had started to fall.

Amber held out her gloved hand to catch the flakes and watch them melt on its surface. "Was it supposed to snow today?"

Wes pressed his palm to his forehead and sighed. "We totally forgot to check the weather."

Jake stared at a dark gray band of clouds that had appeared behind the mountains. "I wonder if the wind is blowing the snow in from those clouds?"

Amber looked up at the darkening sky. "I bet you're right, Jake. We should keep our eyes on it."

They soon came to a sign that pointed to the right and read *Lake Haiyaha 1.3 Miles*. Taking the trail, they immediately found that it was thick with fluffy snow. So, they unstrapped the snowshoes from their packs, fastened them to their boots, and continued their hike toward the lake.

As the trail narrowed, the snow became deeper, and their pace slowed. Amber was in the front. Jake had already stopped himself from saying anything about how tough the hike had become. He saw the look of relief on

Wes's face when Amber turned around and said, "We should probably take a little break."

They sat on some rocks, drank water from their water bottles, and shared a bag of granola.

"I bet we're close to the halfway point by now." Wes took in the aspen forest that surrounded them. "Did you guys notice that we haven't passed a person in a long time?"

Jake *had* noticed. It was weird to be so far away from the sounds of other voices. The deep blanket of snow made everything soft and quiet. "So, if we are halfway, then it should be around 11 o'clock," he said.

Amber looked at her watch. "It's 10:45, but this snow is slowing us down. We should speed things up a bit."

Jake and Wes nodded in agreement though neither was ready to hike much faster. They were already feeling the effects of the altitude and the sting of the cold air in their lungs. Jake's legs were starting to feel a little shaky. But he stood up and did his best to keep up with Amber.

Ten minutes up the trail, they came to a sign pointing the way to Lake Haiyaha. After taking the side trail, they were soon standing along its rocky shore.

Amber rested her hands on her hips. "Wow! This was worth the hike up here. It's beautiful."

Huge boulders were scattered about the shore of the lake. Ice still covered most of its surface, except in the middle, where a deep green circle of water showed through the melted ice sheet.

"This place is cool." Jake took in deep breaths as he scanned the frozen lake. "It really feels like we're in the mountains."

Amber didn't respond. She was watching the sky.

Wes glanced up too. "Looks like more snow is coming, doesn't it?"

"It does," Amber replied. "If it gets worse, we could just skip the side trail to Emerald Lake. That would cut a mile off our trip."

"We can make it," Jake said. "We've just got to get moving." He tightened his snowshoe straps and started hiking back to the trail.

Wes held up his gloved hands. "But we just got here."

Jake's heart beat faster. "We *can't* miss Emerald Lake."

Amber turned to face Jake. "Why not?"

"Just because...I want to see it," Jake tried not to sound as anxious as he felt.

"Is it about your morse code thing?" Wes asked.

Amber heard the words 'morse code' and looked interested. "What morse code thing?" she asked.

"Jake had a note back in his camper that was written in morse code," Wes explained.

"Did you decode it?" she asked.

"We did," Wes answered, "and it said *Emerald Roots*. I

asked Jake what it meant, but he seemed like he didn't want to talk about it."

"I just want to see the lake, okay," Jake really wanted to avoid any more conversation about the clue. "We've already come this far, and I don't want to skip it. So, let's get going."

Amber looked at Wes and whispered, "What's up with him?"

Wes shrugged his shoulders. They put their packs back on and followed Jake. After crossing the creek that flowed out of Lake Haiyaha, the trail became steep again. Gray clouds filled the sky, and the snow was falling in big, thick flakes. More snow covered the path, and their pace slowed. After an hour, they arrived at Dream Lake. Here, a sign with an arrow pointed to *Emerald Lake 0.6 Mile,* and another arrow pointed in the opposite direction that read *Bear Lake 1.1 Miles.*

Wes started to take off his pack to take a break when Jake said in a hurried voice, "It's super close. Let's keep going."

"Wait," Amber interrupted. "This is really important. It's 11:30, and the weather is getting worse. We really need to talk about this and make a good decision, Jake."

"We can totally do this, Amber," he replied.

"Maybe we can, but we need to stop for a minute and make a decision *together.*"

"Okay," Jake relented, but it made him feel even more anxious.

"So, we have to be back by one o'clock, or our parents may not let us do this again." Amber tugged on her gloves.

"And with the snow, they might already be getting worried about us," Wes added.

"I think we can do it." Amber looked at Jake. "But we need to agree that if the snow gets worse, we'll turn back."

"Okay." Jake nodded. "If it gets bad, I *promise* we'll turn around."

As they hiked toward Emerald Lake, the wind picked up, and the snow started to swirl around them. They passed two hikers traveling in the opposite direction.

"It's pretty up there," one of the hikers said. "But be careful. The snow is starting to cover the trail."

"Thanks for letting us know," Jake replied.

"Sure thing," the hiker said. "You guys are close. It's right up ahead."

Emerald Lake

A few minutes later, Emerald Lake came into view. High above its green waters, jagged pinnacles of rock appeared through the snow. Thick fog streamed down the mountainside toward them, and the wind was so strong and cold that it stung their faces. Through the fog and snow, Jake glimpsed the gray limbs of an old tree. He plunged into the biting wind and made his way toward it.

Moments later, he heard his name. "Jake!"

Amber and Wes were calling for him. He looked over his shoulder toward their voices, but everything behind him was enveloped in dense fog. "I'm this way!" he yelled over the gusts of ice and wind. Then, before him, the form of a tree materialized like a ghost in the mist. Its gray and twisted arms had been shaped by years of stormwinds, bending to the east. A few green needles remained in bunches on the tree, proof that the ancient pine was still a living thing.

"Jake!" the voices called again through he fog.

"I'm over this way!"

The two figures emerged from the mist.

"Jake, we have got to go!" Amber's voice sounded angry. "This is getting really serious."

"I just need a few minutes," Jake yelled over the low roar of the wind.

"For what?" she asked.

"I'm trying to find something!"

"Whatever it is, you're not going to find it in this weather." Amber shook her head. "It's getting darker. And you *promised.*"

"Jake, we are getting cold." Wes's voice was shaky. "We really need to head back. Now!"

Jake could now make out the twisted trunk of the pine and could see a web of roots that crawled over the rock and dirt below it. He ran towards it, and Amber and Wes followed.

Amber hit Jake with the back of her glove. "Jake, you're not listening to us."

"I know. I'm sorry. I just *have to find this.*"

Amber grabbed the shoulder of Jake's jacket and pulled him around. "Jake, what is going on? You're putting us in danger. And you're not telling us why."

"It's about the morse code, isn't it?" Wes rubbed his arms, trying to keep warm. "If you are going to make us wait here in the cold, we deserve to know what's going on."

Jake tried to think of how he could keep it a secret, but every option felt like a lie. He had to tell them the truth— at least part of it.

"It's a scavenger hunt. My grandpa left me clues, and the one in morse code led me here."

"So, you think there is another clue hidden somewhere near this tree?" Amber asked.

Jake nodded, still afraid they would think this whole thing was stupid and would make him give up and miss this chance to find the next clue.

"Five minutes." Amber sounded like a teacher demanding all pencils down. "We'll help you look for *five minutes*. After that, we leave—no matter what. Agreed?"

"Agreed," Jake replied. "Thanks, Amber. I'm sorry for..."

"We don't have time for apologies right now, Jake. Just tell us what to do."

"I think there's something hidden behind these roots. Help me dig."

They began scraping the snow away to reveal an even larger web of roots twisting over an area ten feet wide. They reached through the holes between the roots, digging with their gloved hands into the void behind them. Their fingers touched nothing but dirt, rock, and sand.

"Wait, I think I found something!" Wes called out above the sound of the wind. "It feels like glass." He pushed his arm through the roots as far as he could. "It's just at my fingertips." Wes struggled to reach it.

"My arms are longer," said Amber, "Let me try."

Wes moved out of the way, and Amber plunged her hand through the hole.

"I've got it!"

CHAPTER 12

TEAM

She pulled her arm from the roots and snow and opened her hand. "It's an old bottle."

It was made of aqua-blue translucent glass, and the remains of an old cork sealed the top. She held the bottle close to her ear and shook it. "There's something inside." She slid off her backpack, unzipped the main compartment, and placed the bottle inside.

"What are you doing?" Jake demanded.

"I'll give it to you, Jake. I promise. But not until we get back safe and you tell us what's really going on. We don't have time right now to figure out what this is."

"Hey guys," Wes interrupted, "I hate to ask this, but where did the trail go?"

Jake and Amber turned around to see that the snow

had covered everything, including the prints of their snowshoes.

"What time is it?" Jake asked.

"It's noon," Amber answered. "So, we have just one hour to get back."

"It's about a mile and a half." Wes bent down and tightened the straps on his snowshoes. "I think we can do it if we go fast."

"And *if* we can find the trail," Amber added.

Wes had the map out, trying to study it in the falling snow. "The trail goes due east, past Dream Lake. That means if we keep going east, we should be okay." He adjusted his compass and noted the direction.

"Can you lead us?" Amber asked.

"Sure," Wes replied.

They pulled on their packs and followed the compass bearing in the hopes of finding clear signs of the trail. As Jake struggled through the blinding snow, the snowpack below his feet began to sound strange, almost hollow.

"Hey guys," Jake said. "Doesn't this sound kinda weird to you? Because–" Without warning, his legs broke through the snow and the rest of him nearly disappeared into the ground.

"Help!"

Amber and Wes rushed back to find Jake buried up to his neck.

"Are you okay?" she asked.

"Yeah, my ankle is kinda twisted," he groaned, "but I think that it's okay. I feel like I'm hanging in the air."

"I've heard about this," said Wes. "I bet we're in a boulder field, but it's all covered up with snow. You must have fallen into a gap between the boulders."

"Where's that beacon thing?" Amber asked. "We can call for help."

"We don't have time to call for help." Jake tried to keep still so that he wouldn't fall further into the void. "Can you guys dig me out?"

"Yes," she replied, "but we can't risk you slipping further down or one of us falling in too."

Wes chewed on his lip. "I've got an idea. We can dig a space out off to the left. That way, Jake can lie down on his side and keep from slipping further into the hole."

They began to dig, but the snow was more like ice. Amber took off her snowshoe and used its hard edge to break up the compacted snow. Seeing that it was working, Wes pulled off one of his snowshoes and did the same. Within five minutes, they had dug out an area where Jake could now lie on his side.

"I really owe you guys." Jake leaned his shoulder and chest onto the more stable snow. "Sorry to get us into this mess."

"We're a team, Jake," Wes said.

As Amber and Wes worked to dig out his legs, Jake couldn't help thinking how good it felt—even though he was stuck in the snow—to have friends. He hadn't felt like this in over a year. In fact, he had kind of given up on the idea. Just then, Amber was able to move a large chunk of snow out of the way.

"I can move my right leg!" Jake wriggled it out of the snow.

Amber stopped digging. "Do you think that if we can get our hands under your arms, that we could pull you out the rest of the way?"

"I think so. Just be careful not to slip into the crack."

Wes and Amber grabbed Jake under his armpits and pulled. Jake pressed his free snowshoe against the icy ground. He slid up out of the gap, and all three of them fell backward into the snow.

"We did it!" Wes yelled.

Amber laughed in relief. Jake stared up at the sky, grateful to be free. They all stood up and dusted the snow off their jackets and pants.

"Guys, thanks for getting me out. That was pretty scary. I thought I was going to just disappear under the ground."

Amber punched him in the shoulder. "Like Wes said, we're a team." She tapped her watch. "But we lost a lot of time."

"This way." Wes pointed straight ahead. "Just follow right in my tracks so that nobody falls into another snow pit."

Uncle Brian was leaning against the side of the Ranger station at Bear Lake when the three kids came jogging down the trail. "You're late!"

"Jake fell..." Wes began, trying to catch his breath.

"I slipped into..." Jake started to say but couldn't finish. Like Wes, he was recovering from their speed hike back to Bear Lake.

"We had to dig him out." Amber tried to explain, struggling to talk while so winded.

Wes still had his hands on his knees. "It was some kind of snow pit."

Uncle Brian walked up to Jake, put his hand on his shoulder, and looked him in the eyes. "Jake, are you sure that you're okay?"

"I guess so. My ankle got twisted, but I've been running for almost a mile, and it's not hurting much."

"That's good to hear, but I want to take a look at it when we get back to camp." Uncle Brian turned to Wes and Amber. "Why didn't you guys call us or use the beacon?"

"We thought about it, Dad. But Jake was slipping, and we needed to get him out quick."

"Next time, you need to do both. Dig him out *and* turn on the beacon." Uncle Brian took off his sunglasses so that they could see his eyes. "I know you guys were in a tough spot and had to make a fast decision. Now that you're out of it and safe, I want you to learn from it."

"We sure will, Uncle Brian," Jake said.

"Well, let's get you three loaded up in the jeep and back for some lunch. I made chili while you were on your adventure."

The weather was completely different back in Moraine Park. Jake could see the gray clouds still covering the mountains near Bear Lake. But at the campground, the sky was blue again, and it was much warmer. Uncle Brian served up three steaming bowls of chili to the kids, who were sitting at the picnic table behind the Catalinas' camper.

"Guys, I'm really sorry for getting us into that mess."

Jake shook his head and stared at the gray woodgrain surface of the table. "I shouldn't have gone off alone. I wasn't thinking about you guys. Instead, I was just thinking about the clue."

"We could have made a plan to go to Emerald Lake first," Amber replied. "But you didn't tell us."

"Yeah, Jake." Wes shrugged his shoulders and lifted his hands from the table. "Why didn't you tell us?"

Jake could see that Wes was hurt by being left out.

"I guess that I wanted to keep it to myself," he admitted. "It's nothing against you guys. You're both great. It's just that it's all so new. It's something my Grandpa trusted to me, and I feel like I should be able to do it alone."

"Doing stuff alone isn't very fun." Wes raised his eyebrows. "I should know. Nobody at school cares much for the stuff I'm into."

Jake hadn't considered that his cousin might be having a hard time, too. When things got bad at school, Jake was able to talk about it with his brother. Wes didn't have any siblings, and from what Jake had gathered during the last twenty-four hours, his cousin didn't have many friends either.

"Well, it looks like maybe the three of us have something in common." Amber smiled. "All the girls in my class live on their phones. None of them care much for doing stuff like camping and biking—but I love it. And, *you guys love it too.* If we're going to be stuck together for two whole months, we might as well be friends."

"So," Wes began, "it looks like we're a team. And, if you let us in on this scavenger-hunt thing, Jake, then our team is going to have a real mission."

Amber pulled the blue bottle out of her backpack and set it in the middle of the picnic table.

"I'm ready to let you guys in," Jake said. "But you've first got to open that bottle."

Amber pushed the bottle across to Jake. "I was going to let you open it. I mean, it's your clue."

"I think it's *our clue* now." Jake pushed the bottle back to Amber. "Whatever is in that thing belongs to the team. So I think *you* should open it."

Amber smiled, picked up the bottle, and tugged on the cork. But it was so brittle, it fell into pieces with part of it still plugging the opening.

"Try this." Wes offered her his pocket knife. "Use the corkscrew."

Amber turned the corkscrew into the stopper, pulled, and removed it from the bottle. She peered inside. "It's a piece of leather."

Wes took his swiss army knife from Amber, slid a long set of tweezers out from the compartment on its side, and handed them to her. "These might help."

Holding the bottle upside down, she was able to grab the leather with the tweezers. After some twisting and pulling, she finally eased it through the top of the bottle. She slid the scrap of leather across the table to Jake. He unfurled it with his fingers. Scratched into its surface was a message in a very old style of handwriting. It read, *Find the Apache Fort.*

"What do you think that means?" Amber asked.

"It means we need to find the Apache Fort," Wes answered.

"Of course it does, Wes," Amber replied. "I mean, do we just go there and the next clue will magically appear?"

Wes looked at Amber and rolled his eyes. "Jake, can I borrow your map?"

"Sure." Jake dug into his pack and handed the map to Wes, who unfolded it and began searching.

Amber got up and began walking away.

"What are you doing?" Jake asked.

"I'm getting my phone."

Jake leaned over the map and scanned the map with Wes. Moments later, Amber appeared typing something into her phone.

"You guys find it?" she asked.

"Nothing," Wes replied. He pushed the map toward Jake and looked at Amber's phone. "How about you?"

"I've done like five different searches, and there's nothing about an Apache Fort in Rocky Mountain National Park."

"I think we're going to have to go *old school* on this one." Wes squinted and pursed his lips.

"Old school?" Amber replied.

"The library," Wes answered. "We passed one in town when my dad and I went to get food. They probably have a local history section or something like that."

"When I went to grab my phone, I overheard our parents talking about going into town for pizza this week. I bet that I could convince them to go later this afternoon."

"Sounds like a plan." Jake sat up straight. "But first, let me tell you about the scavenger hunt."

"You mean *the mission*," Wes replied.

"Yes." Jake crossed his arms and took in a deep breath. "*Our* mission."

CHAPTER 13

TO THE LIBRARY

"It's going to make more sense if I just show it to you. Follow me." Jake got up from the picnic table and led the way to his family's camper.

But Amber headed in the opposite direction. "I'll be there in like one minute. I want to ask our parents about going into town before they start making other plans."

"Good idea." Jake gave her a thumbs up. "We'll wait for you."

The boys entered the camper, and before sitting down at the table, Jake opened the bench seat. He pulled out the scrapbook and the box, then placed them on the table beside the blue bottle and scrap of leather.

Moments later, Amber opened the door. "They said 'yes'!"

Wes gave her a high-five. "Nice work, Amber!"

"Yeah, thanks," Jake added.

Amber slid into the booth beside Wes. They both got quiet as they studied the items in front of them.

Jake broke the silence. "So, this is it." He put both his hands down on the table. "Right before we left for Colorado, I was visiting my grandma, and she gave me this note that my grandpa had left for me." Jake pulled out the envelope, opened it, and passed it to Wes.

After reading it, Wes furrowed his eyebrows and handed it to Amber, who seemed equally confused.

Jake smiled. "It's a cipher."

Wes's eyes widened, and he snatched the note out of Amber's hands. "Whoa, this is so cool!" He paused, probably realizing just how rude grabbing the note had been. "I'm so sorry. I just got super excited. Ciphers are like my favorite thing in the world."

"Don't worry about it." Amber smiled. "But can I look at it, too?"

"Oh, sure, definitely." Wes moved the note over, and Amber scooted closer so that she, too, could read it.

Jake explained that the cipher led him to the attic, where he found the hidden scrapbook, which turned out to be more than just a treasure of pictures. It contained clues, including the one in morse code that led them to the bottle at Emerald Lake.

Seeing the note in his Grandpa's handwriting sent a

wave of sadness through Jake's body. He recalled the attic. His grandpa's desk, his writing jacket still draped over the back of the chair, open books, and a sharpened pencil. It was as if his grandpa had just stepped away for a moment, perhaps to get a cup of tea, and would soon return. Jake let out a quiet sigh that the other two didn't seem to notice.

Wes set the cipher down, and his mouth fell open. "So, your Grandpa Evans put this whole thing together before he died?"

"He planned this whole trip, too." Jake was now trying to hold back tears. "It looks like it was something that he'd been working on for a really long time. Like for years."

"Wait a minute." Wes leaned forward on his elbows. "You mean that he planned out this entire trip for you as a big scavenger hunt!"

Jake couldn't speak. He nodded, and the hint of a smile spread across his face.

Wes hit the table in his excitement. "That is like the *coolest* thing I've ever heard in my life!" He fell back against the seat cushion, his eyes brimming with wonder.

But Amber's face was solemn. "Jake, I'm sorry to hear about your grandpa. My mom and dad told me on the drive here. They said that it was really unexpected and that it's been pretty tough for you."

Jake glanced down at his hands. "Thanks, Amber."

"Yeah, Jake, I'm sorry too." Wes looked down at the table as he talked, tracing the grain of the wood with his finger. "My parents told me last year, back when it happened. I felt really bad for you 'cause I know you guys were super close."

"Thanks, Wes. We were close." Jake bit his lip, and a tear slipped from his eye. "Sometimes, I just miss him so much. He was the best."

A quiet moment passed between them. Jake went on to show them the picture of the cabin and how it had led him to Jasper and the package.

"What was in it?" Wes asked.

"That." Jake pointed to the old wooden box.

Amber moved her hands toward it but stopped. "Is it okay if I look at it?"

"Sure." Jake pushed it across the table to her.

She picked it from the table and then gently shook the box to get a sense of its weight. "This thing is *way* heavier than I thought it would be. What's inside?"

"I have no idea." Jake shrugged. "I can't find any way to open it."

Amber passed it to Wes, who began looking for some way to open the top. "It's like a puzzle. It's locked, but there's no place for a key." Confounded by the design of the box, he set it back on the table.

"But it gets kinda weird." Jake's voice grew quieter

than before. "Like there's something else going on. I mean, I don't think this is just a game."

"What else could it be?" Amber asked.

"Well, I've been thinking about a few things that just feel strange. Like when I was talking to Jasper, he was acting super suspicious of everything, looking around and whispering. And they used code names."

Wes looked like he was going to explode with excitement. "Oh my gosh! This is just getting cooler every minute." He grabbed his head with his hands. "*Who* used code names?"

"My grandpa, Jasper, and some guy with the code-name Mather–that's the guy who mailed the package to Jasper. And there could be others. They had some kind of ham radio club." Jake went on to explain the old radio system in his grandparents' attic and how it could reach people hundreds of miles away. "But here's the thing: when I asked Jasper more about it, he said it wasn't safe to talk about it."

"That *is* pretty weird." Amber's eyes narrowed, and she leaned back. Her face was saying, louder than words, that she believed him.

"And it gets *weirder*. When I opened the pack, there were instructions inside from Mather. He said to burn the packaging and the note."

"What?" Wes looked confused.

"Yeah, and check this out." Jake plucked the sheet with the instructions from where he had tucked it away in the back of the scrapbook. "It says: *THEY know I have it, and it's no longer safe with me.*"

Amber reached out her hand. "Can I see that?"

"Sure." He handed Mather's note to her.

She read it, then looked up. "So, *They* were after this guy, Mather, who was *The Keeper*. And now you're the new *Keeper?*"

Jake shrugged. "I guess so."

Wes's mouth dropped open. "Jake, that means *they*... could be after *you.*"

Jake laughed. "I don't think so, Wes. I mean, there's no way anyone is going to be following some kid around looking for his family scrapbook."

"Right, but it all depends on what's in *there.*" Wes pointed at the box. "I mean, what if it's a bar of gold, or diamonds, or—I don't know—something like the Sorcerer's Stone, or Maltese Falcon, or a that Rosetta thingy they used to figure out hieroglyphics?"

"What's the Maltese Falcon?" Jake asked.

"Oh, it's so cool. It's this black statue in this old movie that—"

"So, wait," Amber interrupted. "If you're the twenty-fourth *Keeper*, then whatever is in that box is really old, and this whole thing has been going on for a long time."

"Yeah. I told you. It all gets kinda weird."

The three kids sat in silence, looking at the objects on the table, then at each other.

"So that's it." Jake closed the scrapbook. "You guys now know what I know. And the next step is to see if we can figure out the Apache Fort clue."

Wes extended his fist in toward the middle of the table. "To the library!"

Jake and Amber laughed and put their fists in with Wes's, bumped, and pulled them away.

They spent the rest of the afternoon with their parents, wandering through the shops in Estes Park. After they all got ice cream, they gathered along the river walk.

"Do you guys mind if we go off on our own for a bit?" Wes asked.

"How long?" Aunt Judy wanted to know.

"I guess until dinner," Wes answered.

"Okay, just meet us at the pizza place at 5 o'clock," Uncle Brian told them.

"This way." Wes motioned toward Main Street. "I

think I saw some signs for the library." With that, Amber and Jake ran off following Wes.

Before he turned the corner, Jake heard Mrs. Catalina exclaim, "I've never seen kids so excited to find a library." Jake laughed. *If only she knew the adventure we're on.*

The library was located right in the middle of town, so it was easy to find. Once inside, they located the archives and local history section, then split up to search for books about the history of Rocky Mountain National Park.

"I've checked the index in, like, seven books," Amber said, "and *none* of them say anything about the Apache Fort."

"Same here," Jake added. "We've been here for almost an hour, and I haven't found a thing. I'm going to find a librarian."

"Wait, I think I've got something." Wes sat on the floor, surrounded by over a dozen books. Amber and Jake gathered around him. He had been thumbing through a spiral-bound document titled, *Historic Places in Rocky Mountain National Park.* Its pages were yellow from age, and it appeared to have been typed using an old typewriter.

"It says that the Apache Fort wasn't really a fort. It was a rock outcrop that some Apache warriors turned into a makeshift fort by stacking up a bunch of rocks. From up on the outcrop, they could look down on the Ute Indians who were known to use the trail near its base."

"So it was an ambush." Jake leaned in closer to read over Wes's shoulder.

"Yep, they were waiting up there to attack." Wes turned the page. "But the Utes figured it out, ruined their surprise, and won the battle."

"So, does it say anything about where we can find it?" Jake leaned in even closer.

"Um, Jake," Wes said. "You're breathing in my ear."

"Oh, sorry." Jake gave Wes some space.

"It says that the outcrop is near a spring on the western edge of Upper Beaver Meadows. You know, a spring, where water bubbles up from the ground."

"Is that *all* it says?" Jake asked.

"That's it." Wes closed the book. "Hopefully, that's enough to find it."

CHAPTER 14

1880

The bunkhouse came together within the space of a week. Harrison, one of the ranch hands, was also an experienced carpenter and helped Abe build a loft bunk inside. And with scrapwood they purchased from the sawmill in Hiddle Valley, they crafted a small desk to fit underneath.

Abner Sprague had sent a message to Dunraven, resulting in an agreement for the two to meet at noon tomorrow beside the great bend in the creek.

Abe had terrible dreams that night. In all of them, he was being chased. By wolves. By falling rocks. And by Ted Whyte, the man who'd captured him and held him captive in the shed. Abe woke in the morning, cold and covered in sweat. He made his way down to the creek to wash, and after cleaning up in the cool water, he took the artifact out of his pack and scrubbed the dirt from its surface.

He could now see that it resembled an arrow, perhaps a spear. Turning it over, he saw markings. Somehow, deep down inside, Abe understood what they meant. Of course, he couldn't read them—they were in an ancient language of some sort or perhaps were a drawing of something. What he did understand was that the symbols were pointing him *somewhere*, like directions. Standing there, his bare feet in the cool water of the creek, Abe got an idea.

Back at the bunkhouses, Abe held his hand over last night's campfire. It had cooled, so he pulled a piece of charcoal from the center, then went inside, where he lit the kerosene lantern that sat on his desk. He smeared the charcoal over one side of the spearhead. Then tore a piece of paper from his journal and laid it against the blackened silver. Next, he used the edge of the leather journal to press the paper against the object until the markings on the spearhead printed themselves in reverse upon the paper. He did the same with the other side of the object. Abe slipped the first print back into the journal and began to draw. The journal's paper was thin enough to see the charcoal rubbing underneath and sketch the spearhead's outline and strange markings. He did the same with the other rubbing, drawing it onto the next sheet of paper.

It was a few minutes before noon. Abner had given Abe a horse to ride and instructed two of his ranch hands to wait at a safe distance behind them, just in case things went bad. Harrison had left camp ahead of them, galloping his horse towards town. As he and Abner came over the rise, Abe could see Dunraven waiting on the other side of the creek. Insects bloomed from the meadow grass, translucent specks floating in the red light of the rising sun. Dunraven sat straight in the saddle, like the nobleman he was. Beside him was the ranch boss, Ted Whyte. Abe could feel his chest tighten.

"Don't worry, son. I've got a plan." Abner's voice was calm and strong.

Abe could see that Dunraven had his men in the distance, too. Five cowboys sat upon horses behind him on a nearby hillside. He glanced over his shoulder to where Abner's men looked on, the blue-gray and snow-laden mountains stood like a fortress behind them. *Seven against four*, Abe thought.

Abe and Abner approached the edge of the creek, while Dunraven and Whyte, still mounted on their horses, looked down from the high bank on the other side. Abe could now see the fury etched into Ted Whyte's face.

"Give it here, boy!" Whyte shouted, his voice seething with anger.

Dunraven raised his hand to interrupt his foreman.

Abner then nodded to his neighbor and tipped his hat. "Dunraven."

Dunraven returned the one-word greeting. "Sprague. I believe you have something that belongs to me."

Whyte's face was flushed red, and he looked like he was about to burst. "Hand it over–and the boy! He's got a lesson coming. Thieving in this country don't go unpunished!"

Abner remained composed. He ignored Whyte, keeping his eyes fixed on Dunraven. "I've returned the object to its rightful owner."

The nobleman's eyes widened. Dunraven looked back at Whyte. Whyte and Abe gaped at Abner, who continued as if he were a lawyer explaining the case to the judge. "Mrs. Cartwright reported an object missing from her home last week matching the exact description of what this boy found Ted there hiding away in the ground. I thought it only right to send Harrison into town with it this morning."

Hearing this, Whyte yanked the reigns, turning his horse in the direction of town, but stopped when Abner called out his next words.

"You won't catch Harrison. By now, he's already placed the artifact into the hands of Mrs. Cartwright. If it should go missing again, there will be no doubt who took it. And you are right, Ted, thieving in this country don't go unpunished. Now, you and me need to strike a bargain, Dunraven."

Whyte's simmering anger boiled into a fury. He jumped down from his horse and made to cross the creek.

Dunraven held up his hand. "Ted, stop right there." Abe could feel the authority of the man's proper English accent. Apparently, Ted did too, because he halted at the bank of the creek, glaring at Abe. He slid his right hand into his open jacket, where Abe could make out the contours of a leather holster.

"What's your bargain, Sprague?" Dunraven asked.

Whyte looked at Dunraven. From this distance, Abe could see Whyte's confusion and surprise.

"Here's the deal. And you'll take it with no amendment," Abner explained. "I'm not going to report you and your men to the authorities for trespassing on Mrs. Cartwright's property and robbing a widow of her possessions. And you're not going to touch this boy. If I get word that Ted here, or any of your men, come hunting him down or even so much as breathe on 'im, you'll find yourself and Ted here before the judge."

Dunraven fidgeted with the stopwatch in his pocket.

Abner turned to Whyte. "Ted, you've gone and put your employer here in a pinch. A lot of folks 'round these parts ain't so fond of him buying up the valley. This sure would be a good reason to send him back home across the pond."

Whyte's chest heaved, and his hand edged further into his jacket.

Dunraven took a deep breath. "This is a fair bargain. I'll vouch for the boy's safety. And in return, I'll expect this affair will go unmentioned."

Abner tipped his hat to Dunraven. "I expect you to abide by your word."

Abner winked at Abe, and the edge of a smile formed at the corner of his mouth. He turned his horse around, and they began their ride back to the ranch. Abe felt like he had been holding his breath for the last ten minutes, and let out a deep sigh. His body wanted to collapse onto the neck of the horse. Looking over his shoulder, he could see the black silhouettes of Dunraven and his men disappear over the rise. In front of him, Abner rode with the ease of a man who knew exactly who he was and where he was going. And Abe wondered if he stayed long enough, if he too might become such a man.

CHAPTER 15

APACHE FORT

Upper Beaver Meadows was only a short distance from the campground. So, the next morning, Jake, Amber, and Wes handed their parents an itinerary for their hike and walked the campground road north until they found the trail. They followed the path over rocky terrain full of sagebrush and ponderosa pine trees. After a mile, the landscape changed, opening into a spacious meadow.

"This must be it." Wes glanced around. "The book said the Apache Fort was somewhere on the western edge of this meadow."

"And near a spring," Amber added.

"What if we followed the creek?" Jake pointed to the north. "See how it cuts through the meadow right there? At my grandma's farm, they have a spring back in the woods. And the water from the spring makes a little stream that flows down to their creek. If the spring is still here, then I bet it does the same thing." When he pictured the farm, Jake remembered the walks he would take with his grandpa into those woods where they would clean out the leaves and branches that choked the spring's flow. He missed the closeness of those moments, how he could always tell that his grandpa enjoyed being with him.

The three kids followed the creek until they came to a trailhead. Crossing a small footbridge, Amber walked over to read the trail signs that described the area. "Hey, guys, look at this. It says that this trail is the one the Ute Indians took up to the top of the mountains." She pointed it out on the sign.

"So, we've got to be close." Jake scanned the meadow and could see the path Amber had found on the map. "What if we followed the Ute Trail for a bit?"

Amber nodded. "Sure, let's do it."

Jake led them onto the trail as Wes walked along behind them, studying the open map.

"What's that thing over there?" Amber pointed to a small shed tucked away near a stand of aspen trees.

"Looks like an old outhouse." Wes grimaced. "Let's go check it out."

They ran through a field of grass to get to the shed. It was about five feet wide on both sides, eight feet tall, and made of dark brown, weathered wood. The shingles on the roof were worn and peeling away. Wes tried the door. "It's locked. This is strange. Why would someone build a shed out in the middle of nowhere?"

"Wait, I hear something." Jake walked closer to the structure and put his ear against the siding.

Wes and Amber did the same.

"It sounds like water dripping into a pool," Amber said.

"I bet it's a springhouse!" Jake tried to peer between the cracks in the wood siding. "The pioneers would build these around springs to keep animals and leaves and stuff from ruining the water." He turned to face Wes and Amber. "This must be the spring!"

The three turned around to study the landscape. "I wonder if that could be it?" Amber pointed to a copse of pine trees. "It's all covered with trees, but it looks like a rock outcrop like the book described."

They hiked into the trees and scrambled up the rocks, finding their way to the top.

"Wow, you can see forever up here." Jake turned to the west and pointed. "And look, there's the Ute Trail right down there."

Amber and Wes looked to where Jake was pointing and spotted a hiker traveling along the path.

"This would be the perfect place if you were planning a surprise attack." Wes walked over to the edge. "I bet the Apaches piled up rocks right here, laid down behind them, and waited."

"But where do we find the clue?" Amber asked. "I mean, this place is pretty big."

"Maybe it's like the bottle—" Wes scanned the broad stone surface— "hidden inside a crack in the rocks somewhere."

"Let's spread out and look," Jake said. "I'll take this side of the outcrop. Amber, you take the middle. And, Wes, you take the far side over there."

For about twenty minutes, they searched the entire face of the rock but found nothing.

"What if we explore around the base of it?" Amber

suggested. "There's probably more cracks and holes down there."

They scrambled down and began walking around the foot of the Apache Fort. Then, on the north side, on the flat face of one of its cliffs, something came into view.

"Guys, I found something!" Amber yelled. "Come over here! There's writing."

Rock face at edge
of The Apache Fort

Above their heads, on a smooth section of the granite rock, a series of faint numbers and letters were painted in white.

"Whoa!" Wes stared up at the writing. "That's got to be it!"

Jake craned his neck and squinted his eyes. "It's kinda hard to read, but I think we can figure it out." He opened his backpack and pulled out a notebook and pencil. "Amber, can you read it to me?"

"Sure. The first part looks like the numbers eight, four, six, and...a three." She took a step closer to the rock. "Then the letters *US*, followed by *BM*. There's more, but it's harder to make out. It looks like a letter *N*."

Wes stepped alongside Amber and went up on his tiptoes, trying to inch closer to the words. "I think you're right. It's a capital *N*. The next part is so faded, but I think it says, *60FT South*."

"That's what I see too." Amber's eyes narrowed as she tried to make out what came next. "And then there are a bunch more numbers."

"I'm writing it all down." Jake raised his eyes from the paper to study the numbers, but he couldn't make them out. "They're too faded and far away. I wish we had a ladder or something."

"I've got an idea." Wes slipped his pack off his shoulder and began fishing for something. He pulled out a small set of binoculars and focused them on the writing. "Now I'm too close." He ran about ten yards into the woods, turned around, and fixed the binoculars on the cliff face again. "I've got it! It says, *40.433* then *105.7438*."

"What do you think it means?" Amber asked.

Wes scratched his head. "I don't know, but I feel I've seen that number before."

"Which one?" she asked.

"The first one. The one you read out to Jake: *8463*. Here, look." Wes kneeled, pulled out the map from his pack, and unfolded it on the ground. "There is a small X on the map right where we are standing and an elevation number beside it. It's the number: 8463 feet."

"So, it's some kind of elevation record." Jake looked up from the map and back at the white writing on the rock. "But that isn't much of a clue. It just gives us information about *this* place."

"How about the other stuff?" Amber asked. "Maybe the first part is about this location, and the second part is the clue."

Wes raised a finger to the sky. "It could be another cipher...like a letter-number code. You know, where the number one stands for the letter A, the number two stands for B, and so on." Wes put out his hand to Jake, "Can I borrow your notebook?"

Jake gave Wes the pad and pencil. Wes wrote out twenty-six numbers and their corresponding letters of the alphabet. Then he wrote out the numbers and began decoding them. "Most of the time, a zero just gets turned into the letter O, but sometimes with this code, it becomes a space between words. I'm going to try both."

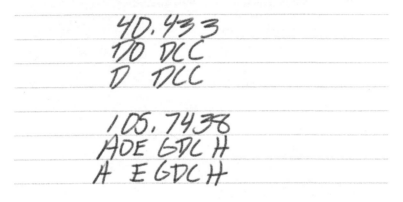

Wes stared at the results. "Well, that looks like a bunch of gibberish."

Jake put his hand on his cousin's shoulder. "Thanks for trying. It was a good idea."

"Wait!" Amber kneeled closer to the map and began inspecting the edges. "Look at these numbers that run along the black borderlines of the map. They look like the ones in the code. See how this one says *105° 30' 00*. It's similar to the 105.7338. And see this one down here along the bottom?" She set her finger beside another set of numbers. "It says *40° 22′ 30.*"

"That's longitude and latitude!" Jake gave Amber a fist bump.

"Right!" Wes smacked himself in the forehead. "Why couldn't I see it? It's obvious. Those are coordinates! And I bet they lead us to the next clue!"

They ran almost the entire way back to the campground. When they arrived, Wes burst into his family's RV to search for something. Moments later, the RVs screen door slammed shut, and Wes emerged with a small black device in his hand.

"Jake, can you read those coordinates to me? I'm going to plug them into this GPS."

"Couldn't we just use a maps app on a phone?" Amber asked.

"I thought about that," Wes replied, "but our reception is so slow here. This will be faster. The GPS works like the beacon my dad gave us. It uses satellite signals to find locations."

Jake read the coordinates out loud. "Forty point four,

three, three, and one, zero, five, point seven, four, three, eight."

Wes punched them into the GPS. "Okay, I've got it!" The hopeful look on his face turned into a cringe. "Oh, no. I've got bad news, guys. The location is five hundred and thirty-four miles from here."

"That's terrible!" Jake's shoulders slumped as he sighed. "How in the world are we going to get *there*?"

Amber looked over Wes's shoulder at the GPS screen. "Maybe it's in another one of the parks we're going to visit? What state is it in?"

Wes began pushing a button to zoom out from the location marker on the GPS. "Looks like it's in...Montana."

"Yellowstone is in Montana." Amber tried to look closer at the screen. "Is the location inside of that park?"

"No," Wes answered. "It's literally out in the middle of nowhere." Wes straightened his back and took a deep breath. "Wait a minute. Jake, can you read those coordinates off again?"

Jake read the numbers aloud a second time.

Wes typed them in slowly. "Yep, I guess I typed one of the numbers in wrong the first time." He grimaced. "Sorry."

Jake and Amber both breathed a sigh of relief.

"Okay, so it's definitely here in Rocky Mountain National," Wes said, "about eight miles away."

Jake grabbed Wes's backpack off the ground and took out his map. He stretched it out on the picnic table, but a gust of wind threatened to blow it away, prompting Wes and Amber to quickly gather four large rocks and set them on the corners of the map to hold it down.

Wes compared the small GPS screen with the map and pointed to the location. "So, it's right off of this super curvy road."

Jake double-checked the coordinates with the numbers alongside the edges of the map. "Yep, that's it: Fall River Road. And the mark on the GPS is right over a place on the map called *Willow Park*."

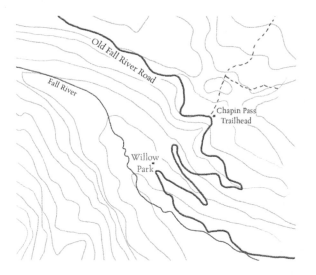

Without saying a word, Wes got up and ran into the RV. He returned with a guidebook. Flipping to the index, he found *Fall River Road, page 128,* then turned to the page about the road. "So, Fall River Road was the first road in the park to go up to the top of the mountains. But it was later replaced by Trail Ridge Road, so not a lot of people drive the old road anymore."

"My parents were talking about us going up to the top of Trail Ridge Road sometime before we leave," Jake said. "Maybe we can take this old road instead."

Wes looked up, worry etched into the creases around his eyes. "How many days do we have left at the campground before we have to leave?"

"After today, we've got two more days here," Jake answered. "So we need to figure this out soon."

"Okay." Wes studied the book again. "It's a dirt road, and it says the road is closed most of the year because of snow."

Amber put her hands on her hips. "So, how are we supposed to get there?"

"Bikes!" Wes exclaimed. "It says here that Fall River Road is perfect for bike riding early in the summer because it's closed to cars until the park service can clear all the snow and repair the road."

"But look, that's like fifteen miles of road, and all of it

is uphill." Amber pointed to the map. "That would be really difficult."

Jake paused to think for a moment. "What if we start at the *top* and coast downhill to Willow Park." He traced his finger along the road to where it ended. "Old Fall River Road and Trail Ridge Road meet here at the Alpine Visitor Center, up at the top of the mountain. What if we ask our parents to drop us off with our bikes, and we ride down?"

Wes looked from the map to Jake. "That's genius!"

Amber tapped her mouth with her forefinger. "Well, now, we just need to convince our parents that this is a good idea."

CHAPTER 16

FALL RIVER ROAD

Uncle Brian rubbed his chin. "So—let me get this straight—you want to bicycle for fifteen miles down a curvy mountain road that may or may not be covered in snow?"

Jake nodded and tried to read his uncle's face.

His serious look split into a smile. "Sounds fun!" Uncle Brian looked over at the other two dads who were sitting in camp chairs and talking. "I'll be right back. I've got an idea."

All three of the kids breathed a sigh of relief. Amber smoothed her hiking pants with both of her hands and said, "I was for sure he wasn't going to let us go."

Moments later, Uncle Brian returned. "We've decided to join you. I'm sure you three want to have your own adventure, so we'll bike down ahead of you."

The plan required them to take two vehicles. Mr. Catalina would drive his truck to the bottom of Fall River Road and park at the nearby Endovalley picnic area. That way, when they finished the fifteen-mile trip down the mountain, they could put their bikes in the back of his truck and return to the campsite. After he finished parking at Endovalley, all six of them squeezed into Mr. Evan's truck to drive the twenty-two miles to the top of Trail Ridge Road.

Jake had no idea the drive would be so captivating. After winding through the thick green forest, the road took them above the tree line into the alpine tundra, where fields of short green grass and white snow stretched for miles over the rolling mountain tops of the park.

Wes stared out the window. He had been speechless for miles. "This is *crazy*! There are no guardrails up here. You could just drive right off the side of the mountain if you weren't careful."

Jake looked out the window and down into a deep valley. Wes was right. There was nothing that would stop a car from plunging over the edge and tumbling down the mountainside. The thought was unnerving.

"They just opened the Trail Ridge Road this week," Mr. Evans explained. "It's closed about half of the year because of the snow. Look at that." He pointed out the window as the truck entered a long hallway of snow plowed to both sides of the road and stacked over fifteen feet high.

They passed the lava cliffs and drove through another cut in the rocks.

Jake saw Amber staring at something. "What's that!" she pointed a finger out the passenger side window.

Mr. Catalina also spotted the big, white wool animals with their sharp, jet-black horns. "Wow, they're either goats or sheep!" He turned to Mr. Evans. "Steve, do you mind pulling over so we can get some pictures?"

"Sure thing." Jake's dad steered the truck into a pullout and parked.

Amber was the first out, followed by Wes, then Jake. "Are they the same as the bighorn sheep we saw the other day?" Amber asked.

"No, the bighorn sheep are a brown color," her dad explained. "These guys are bright white and kinda shaggy."

Wes had pulled out his binoculars to get a closer look. "Yeah, they look really different up close." He handed the binoculars to Amber.

She peered through them. "Their horns are spiky. The sheep we saw on our way in had big, curly horns."

A small brown animal scurried across the rocks beside them and disappeared into the ground.

"Did you see that?" Jake pointed at the rocks. "It looked like a groundhog."

His dad saw it, too. "It's a marmot."

Jake's eyes widened. "Did you say *'marmot'*?"

Wes and Amber both turned to look at Jake. He knew they were thinking the same thing he was: *That word. It was in the instructions from Mather: "All we've learned has been entrusted to the Marmot."*

"That's what I said." Mr. Evans scanned the rocks to see if he could spot the animal again. "They live up here above the treeline. And you're right. They're a kind of groundhog. Some people call them whistle-pigs because of the sounds they make. Listen, and you might hear them."

Sure enough, the marmots started making a cheeping whistle sound.

His dad put a hand on Jake's shoulder. "Reminds me of your grandpa."

"A marmot reminds you of grandpa?"

"Sure does." His dad smiled and rubbed the palm of his hand over his jacket pocket, the one directly above his heart. "He was always whistling. That was why his radio club gave him the handle: *The Marmot.*"

Wes and Amber both stared at Jake. Wes mouthed words to Jake silently: "Your grandpa was *The Marmot!*"

Jake was at a loss for words. He took his hat off and ran his hand through his hair. *Grandpa was The Marmot. Everything we've learned has been entrusted to The Marmot. Everything.*

His dad patted Jake on the back. "Well, it's getting chilly up here. We should get a move on."

They all got back into the truck, and a few minutes later, they were at the top. The Alpine Visitor Center reminded Jake of the Alaskan survival shows his dad liked to watch on the Nature channel. A series of stone buildings looked like they were thawing out from the winter landscape. Snow still covered the sides of the buildings up to the windows. The roof beams were made of long gray tree trunks. Enough snow had melted to expose their spearlike tips. After visiting the gift shop and restrooms, the dads lifted all their bikes out of the back of the truck. The kids found their packs and put on their jackets.

"Okay, we'll meet you at the bottom at noon." Mr. Evans secured the strap on his bike helmet and straddled his bike. "That's plenty of time for you kids to stop at Willow Park. Keep track of the time and don't be late." He tapped the watch on his wrist.

"Got it," Jake said.

As their dads raced off on their mountain bikes, Jake, Amber, and Wes discussed their plan.

Jake had unfolded the map to study it one more time. "So, we go about three miles, then Willow Park should be on the third big curve."

"Cool," Wes replied. "I've got the GPS, so we can check the exact coordinates when we get there."

"All right, let's do this!" Jake mounted his bike and pedaled in the direction their dads had gone.

The dirt surface of Fall River Road was broad and empty, except for the occasional patches of slushy snow. Most of the time, all three of them could ride side-by-side.

"This is the best!" Wes yelled over the breeze. "I already wish we could do this again."

"Me, too!" Amber yelled. She started pedaling faster, tearing through the dirt and pulling far ahead of the boys. She hit a small ramp of dirt at the edge of the road and caught some air.

"Whoa!" Jake said. "She *is* good!"

The boys pedaled faster to catch up. The wind blew through their hair, and their open jackets flapped at their sides.

Amber turned and yelled back, "We're at the curves!" They slowed down and turned into the first curve. Jake was still going really fast, and his back tire started to slip out from under him. Somehow he was able to keep the bike upright.

Amber noticed. "Keep your weight over your back tire," she called out. "Like this." She leaned back over her seat. "That will keep you from slipping."

Jake brought his bike alongside Amber. "How do you know how to ride so well?"

"My dad and I mountain bike a lot at this place near my house," she explained. "It's got a bunch of ramps and stuff."

"Well, you're really, really good."

She smiled. "Thanks."

They came to the third curve, stopped, and parked their bikes in the trees. Wes had brought a bike lock and wrapped it around the three bikes.

"Nobody is going to steal them, Wes." Jake glanced around at the forest and mountains surrounding them. "They would need a car or something. Plus, I bet we are like the *only* people up here."

"I know; it just makes me feel better." Wes turned the dials on the lock, then pulled on the cable to make sure it was secure.

They found a trail that led west into Willow Park. As they entered the woods, they could hear the sounds of a mountain stream. Within a few minutes, the trees gave way to a small clearing and an old log cabin.

Wes was behind Amber and Jake, looking down at the GPS unit's screen so he could follow it to the exact coordinates. Jake turned around to ask Wes how close they were and saw that his cousin was about to step into a giant pile of moose droppings. "Wes, stop!"

Too late.

"Augh!" Wes yelled. "This is not helpful." He walked over to a mound of snow and began sliding his foot around in its cold, grainy surface, working as hard as he could to clean the poop off of his shoe. Amber and Jake looked at each other and tried not to laugh.

Through the dense green spruce trees, Jake caught sight of what appeared to be a building. "Come on." He beckoned Amber toward it, and they soon were standing in front of a long, narrow rectangular cabin. It was a long log structure on a stone foundation. Three windows let light inside, and two sets of wood stairs led to two doors. The windows were set too high in the walls for the kids to look inside.

Wes had cleaned off his shoe and continued following the GPS, stopping at the side of the cabin. "This is it!" He leaned against the log structure. "This is exactly where the coordinates lead us."

Jake tried the doors. "It's all locked up."

They walked around the cabin to see if they could find another way in but had no luck. There were other buildings, including an old stable, so they explored the area to see if perhaps the clue was tucked away nearby. Giving up on their search, they sat down at a picnic table, and Amber took out some snacks from her backpack. "Let's take a break and think," she said.

Wes stared at the cabin. "I bet I could find a way to break in–but I think we'd be committing a federal offense. It's government property, you know."

"Yeah," Jake said between bites of beef jerky, "that would be a really bad idea. Let's try not to get arrested today."

They heard the distant thrum of an engine, and all three looked out toward the road. Through the trees, they could see a white truck had come to a stop at the side of the curve.

Amber's eyes narrowed. "I thought the road was closed?"

The engine noise stopped, followed by the thuds of two doors closing. A couple of minutes later, two park rangers emerged from the trees.

Wes looked at Jake and Amber and whispered, "Why do I always feel like I'm in trouble when people in uniforms show up?"

"Maybe it's because you stepped in that moose poop." Amber gave him a serious look. "It's a federal offense, you know."

"Ha, ha." Wes gave Amber a courtesy laugh, but glanced at Jake as if to say, *She's joking, right?*

The two rangers who entered the clearing–one a woman about their parents' age and the other a younger man with a short black beard–seemed surprised to see a group of kids this far up the road by themselves. "We were wondering who those bikes belonged to," the man said. His gray-blue eyes were vigilant, and to Jake, a little unnerving. "How are you kids doing?"

"Good," Wes replied. "We were just stopping here to have some snacks. Is that okay?"

"You guys are just fine." The woman ranger adjusted her hat that sat atop her long, brown braided hair. "We came up here to check the road before we open it up next week. We thought we'd also stop in and make our early summer report on the conditions here at the patrol cabin. Would you guys want to take a look inside?"

All three kids sprang to their feet. "Sure." "Definitely." "Yes."

The woman ranger's smile revealed a set of dimples. "Wow, I had no idea you'd be so interested. It is a cool place, though, and it contains a lot of history. I'm Ranger Wallace, and this is Ranger McDaniels."

The three kids introduced themselves and then followed the rangers to the cabin. Ranger McDaniels opened the door. "Welcome to the Willow Park Patrol Cabin, built in 1923 to serve the workers who were building Fall River Road."

Wes stepped inside first. "Whoa, this place is amazing! It looks like something right out of an old Western movie."

Their footsteps echoed on the room's wood-planked floors. A metal wood-burning stove stood on one side along with cooking utensils, a couple of blue, enamel-coated buckets, and a locked cabinet.

"We're going to head outside to inspect the outbuildings." Ranger Wallace said. "We'll be back in a few minutes. Feel free to explore."

"Thank you," Amber replied as the rangers stepped out the door.

There was something strange sitting on a thick shelf along the back wall: a sculpture made of twisted tree roots, carved into a figure with a walking stick. The figure's head was turned as if he were looking back over his shoulder, and his long beard flowed down to his feet. Someone had carved words into the thick shelf below the sculpture: THE OLD MAN OF THE MOUNTAIN WHO LEADS YOU ON.

A series of images flashed through Jake's mind. The scrapbook. The photo that wouldn't budge. The hidden envelope. The message

"Guys! This is it." Jake motioned for Amber and Wes to join him. "Check this thing out!"

Wes and Amber stared at the strange woodcarving and the message on the shelf.

"In the scrapbook, I found a clue that said to find the Old Man of the Mountain. And that he would show the way."

"Well, that's kinda confusing because he's walking that way–" Amber pointed to the north– "but he is looking in the opposite direction." She pointed to the south.

Meanwhile, Wes was running his finger along a thin groove carved into the shelf. The line had been tinted red with paint and ended with an arrow that pointed south.

He followed the arrow to the end of the shelf, then noticed that a similar groove was carved into the floor. Wes got down on his hands and knees and ran his fingers along the red-tinted line that now ran across the floorboards. "Jake, Amber, come down here. That same kind of red line on the shelf is carved into the floor here, too. And look here...where it ends...there's another arrow and some numbers."

They got down on the floor with Wes.

"What are the numbers?" Jake asked.

Amber found the figures and read them out loud. "Eight-seven-eight-nine."

"I've got a crazy idea." Jake held out his hand to Wes. "Could you give me the map?"

"Sure," He pulled the map out of his backpack. "But

we should hurry up with this before the rangers come back."

Jake unfolded the map and began searching for their location. He found it, pulled a mechanical pencil out of his pack, and marked it with an X. "Wes, can you show me how to line the map up with the compass?" While waiting for Wes to answer, something wafted over him, an odor that made Jake screw up his nose and cringe. "Oh my gosh, what is that smell? It's terrible!"

"It's Wes's shoe." Amber snickered.

"Hey, at least it's just moose droppings. I could have stepped in something worse, like bear poop."

Wes lay the compass down at the top corner of the map, and then he adjusted the dial. After finding north, he rotated the map on the floor until the compass rose on the map lined up with his compass.

"Okay, this might just be a wild guess," Jake said, "but maybe this arrow on the floor will point us to a spot on the map." He paused. "Just watch." Keeping the map oriented to true north, Jake slid the map until the cabin's location matched up with the red channel. He ran his fingernail along the surface of the map, gently pressing it into the channel in the floor and making a crease in the paper. Then running the pencil along the seam he had just created, Jake traced a line across the map. "Read me those numbers again," he said.

Amber found them under the edge of the map, carved into the floor, then read them out again, "Eight-seven-eight-nine."

"This is it!" He crowed. "The line crosses right over the top of something that is marked at 8,789 feet in elevation."

Wes read the name of the location out loud: "The Twin Owls." He looked up at Jake. "That was brilliant!"

"I learned it from you, Wes." Jake patted his cousin on the back. Then he scrunched up his face with a look of disgust. "You've got to do something about that shoe. It smells awful."

CHAPTER 17

1880

Abe woke to the sounds of the ranch hands gathered around the fire to cook breakfast. He rubbed the sleep out of his eyes, dressed, and joined the men. Harrison, still in his long underwear, stood shaving. It was Burly Gypsum's morning to cook. The man was the same age as Albert Sprague, soft-spoken and observant. His copper hair and beard were a marvel to Abe.

"Boys, looks like it's going to be a splendid day in the valley. Might get a touch of rain up there, though." Burly gestured toward the high peak in the distance.

"Does the mountain have a name?" Abe asked.

"Longs Peak—but Hank March says it's got a true name, an ancient name." Burly continued staring at the snow-capped peak, perhaps enchanted by how its massive shape loomed over the landscape.

"Who's Hank March?" Abe asked.

The men all laughed—not at Abe, but at how difficult it was to explain such a curious character like Hank March.

"Imagine a man in buckskin," Burly began, "emerging from the woods with a rifle slung over his shoulder, a beard full of moss and lichen, and feet tough as leather from miles of stalking game."

Harrison chimed in. "Hank knows the names and ways of these mountains like nobody else 'round here. He's gone traipsing about with the Arapahoe and Ute, learning the unwritten stories of these parts."

Abe's thoughts returned to the symbols on the spearhead, now drawn into his journal, and he wondered if perhaps this mysterious mountain man could make sense of them.

"Where do you find him?" Abe asked.

The men laughed again, then Burly explained, "Nobody can find Hank March. He's a rambler. He finds *you*."

Disappointed, Abe sat down on one of the big logs that circled the campfire.

"Hey, kid, sounds like you and the boss have got a

ramble of your own today." Burly flipped several hotcakes out of the cast iron pan and onto a big metal plate.

"Yes, sir. Mr. Sprague says we're going to mark a trail to the top of the peak."

"That's for men braver than me," Burly replied. "Two years back, a fella got clean blown off a ridge up there."

"How?" Abe asked.

"By the mountain itself," Burly answered. "Mountains ain't piles of rock, Abe. They've got a life of their own, stirring up their own weather and shaking off anything that don't belong." Burly threw a slab of bacon into another big cast iron pan, where it began to sizzle and pop. "I don't mean to scare ya. I just mean to say that mountains like Longs Peak, they demand our respect."

Longs Peak

Abe looked again at the mountain, its ridgeline tinted

pink by the first light of the sunrise. Spindrift, like a ghost, blew from the top and spun like a red fire into the sky. Rubbing a thumb against the palm of his hand, he tried not to think about what it might take, or what might happen, on the way to the top.

CHAPTER 18

SURPRISES

"Um, guys, we really need to go." Amber stood above the boys looking at her watch. "I hate to tell you this, but we kinda lost track of time."

Still kneeling on the floorboards, Jake was hunched over the map, trying to figure out how they would get to the Twin Owls. *It's on the other side of town. Maybe we could bike there?* He felt a tap on his shoulder.

"Jake." Wes gestured up to Amber. Her face looked serious, and she was tapping her watch. *Tapping her watch.* The image immediately reminded Jake of his dad telling them to meet at noon. *Keep track of time, and don't be late.* Jake cringed. "What time is it?"

"It's 11:47." Amber winced.

Jake snapped up the map and jumped to his feet. "Shoot! We've got to go."

They ran out of the cabin and waved goodbye to the rangers returning from their inspection of the outbuildings. "Thanks!" they all yelled. Jake felt like they were perhaps being rude by leaving so abruptly. They got to the bikes, and Wes began turning the dials of the combination.

Jake held his forehead and paced. "I can't believe this. We've only got *one* more day here—one chance to get to whatever we need to find at Twin Owls. If we're late–" he shook his head– "there's no way my parents are going to let us go anywhere tomorrow." He looked down at Wes, who was still working on the combination. "What's taking you so long?"

Wes looked over his shoulder at his cousin. "I kinda... um...kinda forgot the combination."

Jake gave Wes a blank stare. He wanted to say, "Are you kidding me? Can't you remember *four* numbers?" Instead, he turned around and continued pacing.

Amber had pulled the map out of Wes's backpack and was trying to figure out how many miles they had left. She exhaled. "Right now, it looks like we're going to be about twenty minutes late."

Jake's anxiety amped. "Wes, could you hurry up," he said through gritted teeth.

"I'm trying!"

Jake noticed the distress in his cousin's voice. He took

in a couple of deep breaths, then squatted beside him. "Sorry. I'm just worried. It's not your fault."

"Thanks."

"But could you hurry up?" Jake smiled, and Wes elbowed him hard enough to throw him off balance. Jake put out his hand to keep from falling over, and it squished into the gray mud. "Ugh!" He wiped it off on his pant leg.

"Got it!" Wes unwound the cable from the bikes, coiled it up, and fastened it into the retaining clip on his bike's frame. They jumped on the bikes and began pedaling hard.

Wildflowers bloomed at the edges of the forest. With each mile, more snowmelt filled the streams that flowed into Fall River. Its waters gushed over rocks and through the ravines alongside the road. Jake felt like they were racing the river to the bottom.

The soft, wet dirt of the road soon became more and more saturated by meltwater. Mud sprayed from their tires and splattered their pant legs and jackets. Puddles filled the road. At first, they tried to avoid them. Then Amber shot straight through an enormous one, drenching her clothes and sending a spray of water high into the air. "It cleans off the mud!" she yelled over her shoulder. The boys followed and were soon drenched from head to toe.

They had traveled a few miles when Jake heard a crash in the woods. From his left came the sounds of branches snapping. Then something big and black trudged out of the trees and into the road. All three kids slammed on their brakes, their back tires fishtailing until they came to a stop.

A moose calf stood in the middle of their path. They were close enough to see its belly rise and fall as it breathed. The forest echoed with more crashing sounds. Another dark mass lumbered out of the woods and down the gravel berm to stand beside its baby.

Without a word, the kids dismounted their bikes and began backing them up. The cow moose looked at them and made a huffing noise.

"This isn't good." Wes looked to Jake, then to Amber. "Mama moose plus baby moose equals super dangerous."

"What do you mean?" Jake asked.

"They get super protective about their babies—like *way* more than most animals."

"What would she do then?" Amber asked.

"Trample us," Wes said. "Guys, I really don't want to be moose-trampled today."

"Me either," Amber replied.

As they continued their slow backward walk up the muddy road, the mother moose just stood there watching them. She let out a wet snort.

"I can't believe this," Jake said. "We're already late, and now a moose is blocking our path."

"At least we'll have a good excuse." Wes made a nervous smile and shrugged his shoulders.

The baby moose began walking, making its way across the road. But mama moose stayed put. She stared at the kids with large brown eyes. Behind her, thick gray clouds had filled the sky. Drops of water began to patter the shoulders of Jake's jacket. Then the calf plunged down the slope toward the creek. Seeing her baby was safe, the giant moose turned and clomped across the dirt road, splashing through a puddle as it went. A moment later, it was out of sight.

The kids jumped back on their bikes and pedaled as fast as they could. The road curved away and downhill into clouds of thick fog. With every crank of their pedals, the rain fell in bigger drops.

They pedaled faster, but the wind was blowing the rain sideways now, sending blasts of water into their faces. The fog, rain, and thickening mud around their tires conspired to slow them down. Jake stood from his seat and cranked harder, but it didn't seem to make a difference.

They shot by a brown sign that read *Chasm Falls* and could hear the thundering water from the road. But they didn't stop. As they passed the roaring sound, Jake looked back to see the river press its way through a fracture in the bedrock and launch a torrent of white water into the air. Mud-covered and soaked, they pedaled on.

A few minutes later, they came to a gate that marked the bottom of Fall River Road. They walked their bikes around it and onto the black asphalt road that led into the Endovalley picnic area. Tall spruce and fir trees caught and softened the falling rain. Mr. Evan's truck was parked in a pullout, and the other dads were sitting on its tailgate. Jake saw his dad's look of relief. Then he pulled back the sleeve of his rain jacket and checked his watch. Jake felt sick to his stomach.

"Whoa," Uncle Brian exclaimed, resting his hands on his hips. "Where did these mud creatures come from?"

Jake looked at his friends. Mud was caked in their hair, covered their shirts and pants, and the rain had done little to clean them up.

Jake's dad's voice wasn't nearly as lighthearted. "You're *thirty* minutes late. We were getting really concerned about you guys."

"We ran into a moose." Wes tried to explain. "Well, we didn't run into it. That would have been really bad. It just was blocking the road."

"There were two of them," Amber added. "And the rain slowed us down, too."

Jake tried to read his dad's face. He looked both concerned and relieved. Was he mad? Jake wondered if he should just let the excuses do their work. But this was the second time they had been late. He hadn't held up his side of the bargain, and now he could feel it: his freedom slipping away.

"It's my fault," Jake blurted out. "We were exploring the cabin, and I lost track of time. Wes is right; the moose slowed us down. So did the rain. But we could have made it on time if I had been paying attention like I promised."

Everyone stayed quiet. Amber and Wes were watching Mr. Evans to see how he would respond, but his face was blank. Jake knew that wasn't a good sign.

Mr. Evans gestured toward the truck and broke the silence. "Let's load up the bikes."

After loading the bikes, the kids took off their muddy jackets, and Mr. Evans laid a blanket down on the back seat of the truck. All six of them squeezed inside and they made their way back to the campground.

The rain had stopped but the clouds had stayed, enveloping Moraine Park Campground in a shroud of mist. The kids had showered, dressed in warm clothes, and were wearing puffy jackets to keep warm. Amber sipped on a mug of hot tea while Jake rubbed his hands together to keep them warm.

"They're not going to let us go anywhere tomorrow." Jake shook his head and sighed.

Wes had his knees on the picnic table bench and leaned over the map, tracing the roads that would take them to Twin Owls. He finished calculating the miles and looked up at his cousin. "You don't know that for sure."

"When my dad gets quiet like that, Wes—that means he's not happy."

"Well, he can be upset and still let you go." Wes scribbled something into a notepad. "Are you just going to give up?"

"I'm not giving up. I'm just being realistic."

"Well, being *realistic* means that we've still got a chance." Wes kept writing in the notebook. "But we've got *zero* chance if we don't make a plan and give our parents an itinerary for Twin Owls."

"I should have been watching the time." Jake held his head in his hands then let them drop to his side.

Amber sat down beside Wes, cradling the steaming mug of tea in her hands. "Jake, we all lost track of time. The *team* lost track of time. That's how the team works: We don't let one person take the blame; we all own it *together*."

Amber's eyes told Jake that it was not worth arguing with her. She believed every word she'd just said.

"Done!" Wes flicked his pencil into the air and caught

it. "I'm going to give the itinerary to my dad. You guys good with that?"

Jake and Amber nodded, and Wes walked into the mist to find his dad.

They spent the rest of the day playing card games and watching the elk at the edge of the meadows. Later in the afternoon, the clouds receded and the sun warmed the rain-drenched tall grass that covered Moraine Park. Wes and Uncle Brian gathered their fly-fishing gear and invited Jake and Amber to join them down at the stream. They taught them how to spot trout along its banks and how to cast a fly. As the sun set, the whole valley turned pink and orange. The elk slowly moved upstream, out of the meadows and into the aspens to bed down for the night. A hatch of insects hung in the air. While the kids attempted to catch one more trout, Uncle Brian sat down to enjoy the twilight. Jake reeled his line in and sat down beside him. Together, they watched Amber and Wes, their playful silhouettes and the glint of gold light illuminating their fly line in the sunset.

Uncle Brian slapped Jake on the back and hugged him

around the shoulders. "Doesn't get much better than this, kid."

"It might." Jake looked at his uncle and smiled. "I mean, we've got almost two months together in places like this. Who knows? It might get better."

Uncle Brian laughed. "Sometimes you remind me of your Grandpa Evans. That's just like something he would've said."

Jake gazed at the sunset and soaked in his uncle's words. Something in his spirit brightened. Wes and Amber had stopped fishing and were walking back with their gear, talking and laughing. He couldn't hear their words, but Jake could tell they were happy and absorbed in the moment just as much as he was.

"I've got good news for you three." Uncle Brian pulled off his sunglasses. "I talked with the other parents, and we'd like to talk with you kids about your itinerary after dinner."

Jake looked at Wes, hoping that he might know more, but Wes just shrugged.

"Well, speaking of dinner, I'm going to go help your mom out." Uncle Brian dusted off his jeans and stood up. "Wes, can you help Jake and Amber pack up the gear?"

"Sure thing, Dad."

Uncle Brian crossed at a shallow spot in the creek, walking across a set of stepping stones.

"So, you don't know what they decided?" Jake asked Wes.

Wes shook his head and gave Jake a blank look. "I've got no idea."

After dinner, Mr. Catalina built a fire, and Mr. Evans asked everyone to gather their camp chairs around the fire ring. Jake, Wes, and Amber sat side-by-side and waited quietly, like a group of defendants in court, waiting for the jury's verdict.

Jake's dad was the first to speak. "When you three were late today, we all got quite worried."

Wes bit his lip and nodded.

"It's not about being on time. It's about your safety and our ability to trust you. Letting you do things on your own comes with some risks. And our families have talked a lot about it: whether or not you're really old enough to be venturing out alone. We decided you were. And we talked with you guys the other night about how important it was to build trust."

Jake sat up in his camp chair and leaned in toward the fire. *This doesn't sound like it's going to turn out very well.*

Uncle Brian talked next. "You've been late twice." He held up two fingers. "We realize that there were some things outside of your control, like the snow that first time, and moose and rain today. But that's kinda the point: you've got to plan for things to go sideways, for surprises."

Jake's dad held the itinerary in his hands. "When we got your plan for tomorrow–to be honest–we weren't sure what to do." He looked at Jake for a moment. "But as we talked about it, we kept coming back to you–" he pointed across to fire at Jake " –and how you took responsibility for arriving late. You could have blamed it on the circumstances, or even made something up–but you told the truth."

"That tells us we can give you three another chance," Uncle Brian said. "We've officially approved your plan to visit the Twin Owls."

Jake felt like he was going to collapse with relief.

"Our only request is that you add your bike route to the itinerary so that we know the exact roads you'll be taking."

"And..." Jake's dad added, "we want you three to be mindful of cars when you're on the roads. You've got to assume..."

Jake finished his dad's sentence, "...that they can't see you."

His dad smiled and nodded. It had been something his dad said to him every time he went on a bike ride.

Wes was sitting upright with his hand raised high, like he was in class.

Uncle Brian noticed and responded. "Yes, the gentleman with the wild, curly red hair."

"Um, the itincrary says that we'll be back by 2 PM."

"Yeah?"

"Let's change that to three—just in case there are some *surprises*."

Hearing the word "surprises," Jake felt a strange sense of warning pulse through his body. He watched Wes give Amber a high five, and couldn't help smiling. But the unsettled feeling stayed. Something about tomorrow felt different, felt dangerous.

CHAPTER 19

TWIN OWLS

The chill of morning was still in the air when they left on their bikes. Jake felt uneasy. But he dismissed the nervous tension that was buzzing in his legs. From the campground, they rode into town, where they stopped at a shop to buy penny candy. Then they followed the riverwalk to a bike path that led them out of town.

Soon they were on a country road headed north. In front of them, a knobby range of gray bluffs towered over the rolling meadows of old ranch lands. The native people named it *Lumpy Ridge* because of its enormous rounded rock cliffs. The rock faces in this part of Rocky Mountain National Park were famous for their rock climbing routes. Some of the best climbers in the world traveled thousands of miles just to spend a few days climbing the granite walls and buttresses of Lumpy Ridge.

"There it is!" Wes pointed straight in front of them. "The Twin Owls."

A gray rock formation stood out from the ridge. The massive stone towers were shaped like two owls nestled close together on their perch. The kids steered into the Lumpy Ridge Trailhead. Wes began securing their bikes to the bike rack while Amber and Jake studied the trailhead signs.

Twin Owls

"Hey, Wes, are you about ready?" Jake called out.

"Just forgot my combination." Wes was bent over, fiddling with the lock. "Don't worry. I'll remember it. Just give me a minute."

Amber noticed that a man waiting by the restroom

kept looking over toward Wes and the bikes. "That guy doesn't look like much of a hiker."

"What do you mean?" Jake asked. "He looks normal to me."

"Take a second, and just look at him."

"That would be weird." Jake fidgeted with the straps on his backpack. "He is going to notice if I'm staring at him."

"Just pretend to tie your boots or something, and then glance over at him." She motioned with her head toward the man.

Jake bent down, double-knotted the laces of his hiking boots, and looked at him. He wore dress pants, a jacket–the kind Jake's dad would often wear to work–and a pair of sunglasses. "He's probably just a tourist stopping to take in the view."

Amber kept her back to the man. "Look at his ear." She raised her eyebrows and whispered. "He's got an earbud in. And he's been talking with someone."

"Amber, he is probably just on the phone with a friend or something." Jake took off his backpack, intending to pull out some of the candy they had bought in town and share it with the other two.

"But he keeps looking over at Wes," she said through clenched teeth.

"Well, Wes is kinda unusual. The crazy red hair gets

people's attention." Jake unzipped the front compartment of his backpack while Amber stole another glance at the man.

Her eyes grew big. "I think he just repeated Wes's lock combination to whoever he's talking to on the phone."

Jake stopped looking for the candy, and his eyes narrowed. "Amber, that's the weirdest thing ever. You're acting paranoid." The word *paranoid* made him stop short, and he immediately thought of Jasper. *It reminds me of the way Jasper eyed the door and looked around suspiciously when he gave me the package*, Jake thought.

"I swear," Amber whispered. Her face was as serious as the gray stone of the Twin Owls.

Wes approached. "Why are you guys whispering?"

Amber gave Jake a stern look then turned to Wes. "Is your lock combination two-five-seven-two?"

Wes's mouth hung open in amazement. "How did you know? And why am I whispering?"

Amber punched Jake in the shoulder.

"Ah, that actually hurt this time." Jake held his hand on the spot where she had hit him.

"It was supposed to. See, Jake. I told you." She glared at him, grabbing a strand of hair from the front of her face and placing it behind her ear.

"Told him what?" Wes's eyebrows furrowed as he leaned in.

"That guy over there is on the phone with someone," she whispered. "He's been watching you dial in your combination, and I watched him say *two-five-seven-two* to the person on the phone."

Wes turned around and stared at the man. Jake grabbed him by the shoulder and turned him back around. "You can't be so obvious!" Jake whispered. He could feel Amber staring at him, waiting for him to admit that she had been right. He looked up from the ground and met her eyes. "I'm sorry. I believe you now."

"He's going into the restroom." She motioned with her head towards the bikes. "Go, quick! Change the combination."

Wes ran to the bikes and began fingering the combination until it was reset. He ran back to Jake and Amber before the man returned.

"Okay, let's get moving," Jake started running up the trail with Wes and Amber at his heels.

After about five minutes, they were winded and slowed to a fast walk.

"Why would that guy want to steal our bikes?" Wes put both of his hands on the back of his head.

Jake glanced at the trail behind them to see if they had been followed. A chipmunk scurried across the gravel path. He stopped and took a deep breath. He looked back down the trail again. *Now I feel like Jasper*, he thought. He pinched his lip as he considered what had just happened. "Guys, I wonder if it's *them*."

Wes's already big eyes grew enormous. "You mean *them*? As in the guys that Mather's note talked about."

Jake nodded. He slowly repeated the line from the note. "THEY *know I have it, and it's no longer safe with me.*"

A cold wind kicked up a cloud of gray dust from the trail. It blew dead leaves out from under the nearby scrub oaks, and they skittered across the ground like pieces of brittle brown paper.

Amber rubbed her shoulders and shivered. "This is getting *real*. We should keep moving. Hopefully, that guy will waste enough time with the bike lock that we can ditch him."

Wes looked down at his shirt. "I should have worn my camo jacket today. Why did I wear orange?" His shoulders fell, and he let out a sigh. "I mean, that's what hunters wear to stand out!"

Amber looked down at her purple shirt, and Jake touched his bright blue one. "We've got to get out of sight, and fast!" Jake said. They resumed hiking but picked up their speed as they went up the trail.

Minutes later, they arrived at the base of the Twin Owls. The giant stone birds peered down at them. Granite boulders were strewn about the ground. Pine trees and

scrub oak brought splotches of green to the rocky landscape and dense cover for the wildlife that lived at the base
of the owls. And here, the trail split.

Jake pulled out his map. "I think we need to get back
in *behind* the Owls by going into one of these two
ravines." He pointed to two valley-shaped areas on the east
and west sides of the Owls. Just then, they heard the
crunch of boots on gravel in the distance.

"There's no time to think about it. Let's just go this
way." Amber pointed to the left, where the trail bent to
the west. They ran.

Still running, Jake scanned the edges of their path.
"There wasn't a trail on the map. Not one that leads to the
rocks."

"There's got...to be a...social trail." Wes took in deep
breaths as he ran.

"What's a social trail?" Amber asked.

"It's a trail that's...not on the map...that people make...
when they... go exploring," Wes panted. "Because people
climb here...there's got to be one."

"There!" Jake pointed to the right. "I see one leading
into the ravine."

A faint path led into the rocks alongside the trail then
disappeared into the dark, forested and narrow pass. They
followed its course as it twisted down, then back up
toward the Twin Owls. The trail was steep now, running

over rock and loose gravel until the path ended at the smooth cliff face below the broad and long chests of the owls.

"We're not going to climb this thing, are we?" Wes asked.

"No," Jake shook his head. "We don't have the gear for that. Remember the big cracks we could see from the road?"

Wes and Amber nodded as they caught their breath.

"That's what we need to look for, some kind of opening in the rock." Jake stared up at the cliffs.

"The trail keeps going here." Amber pointed out a narrow path that curved around the cliff face. They followed it until they came upon an immense gash in the stone and a ramp of boulders leading up and into a space between the two owls. Amber took the lead. "Be careful," she called back. "It would be easy to knock a rock loose and hit the person behind you."

The higher they scrambled up the ramp, the darker it became, the stone walls growing closer together with each step. Jake opened his backpack and pulled out his headlamp. Wes did the same. Soon they came to a space where the rock leveled off. Here, a long, dark crevice ran straight into the heart of the owls. Jake shined his head-lamp into the darkness. "This thing goes *way* back in there."

"Guys," Wes interrupted, "I think we've been followed."

Jake and Amber looked back toward Wes. From this vantage point, they could see the Rocky Mountains and the entire valley of Estes Park. And directly below them, they could make out the main trail, where a figure wearing dark sunglasses stood in the open, staring up at the owls.

"Do you think he can see us?" Wes asked.

"I don't think so. It's so dark in here," Amber said.

"Darn!" Jake exclaimed. "We've got our headlamps on!"

Immediately, Jake and Wes covered the lights with their hands.

"Hopefully, he didn't see us." Jake exhaled with frustration at having made such an obvious mistake.

"I didn't bring my headlamp." Amber shook her head in regret. "Jake, you're going to have to lead us in." She pressed her body against the rock to let Jake in front of her.

"Are there going to be bats in there?" Wes asked.

Jake was already several steps into the crevice and looked up. "Yeah." His voice made a muffled echo as he walked in further. "There definitely are bats in here."

CHAPTER 20

THE CREVICE

Jake watched Wes step inside and look up, shining his headlamp on the bats. Clinging to the walls high above him, the bats slept with their wings draped around their bodies. "I'm so glad they're nocturnal," Wes whispered.

The crevice ran all the way to the top of the Owls, where a sliver of sunlight broke through. Little of the sun's rays reached the bottom, so they continued with their headlamps. Behind him, Jake could hear Wes talking to himself under his breath. "Just don't freak out. Just don't freak out."

"Wes, are you okay?" Jake called back.

Wes sighed. "Yes, I just don't like bats. They remind me of rats–but with wings."

Jake and Amber both snickered.

Wes kept moving, but with his headlamp shining on the bats. "Plus, their poop is like black, greasy, goo."

Amber screwed up her face at the disgusting thought. Jake paused for a moment and waited for Wes to catch up.

Fine dust covered the narrow path below their feet. Except for their footprints, there were no tracks or other signs that a human had been this way in years. The cool, musty space reminded Jake of a crypt, and he felt like they might be intruding upon the site of an ancient tomb. He kept walking, and the crevice walls grew closer together until they almost blocked the way. Jake stopped, sucked in his belly, and squeezed through the pinch. Amber and Wes did the same. They followed the path before them as it curved away into deeper darkness. Then Jake halted. It was a dead end.

"What do we do now?" Wes asked.

Jake was studying something. "Guys, look at this." He rubbed his hand against a smooth patch of the rock wall. "See how the rock looks different here? It's like someone patched this wall with cement."

He picked up a stone from the floor and tapped at the surface. It was thin and hollow. Jake struck harder with the stone until he was able to punch a small hole through the cement. Once he had made the hole big enough, he reached his hand into the gap. His fingers found a metal object. Grabbing hold of it, he tried to pull it through the hole, but the opening was too small. He picked up the stone again and pounded away at the edges until the hole was big enough. Jake reached his hand in again and pulled out a rusted metal container, rectangular in shape, and just bigger than Jake's hand. Amber and Wes leaned in to get a better look. Jake shook it. "There's something inside." He tried the lid, but rust had sealed it shut, so he turned it over. "There's something scratched into the bottom. But it's too dirty. I can't read it."

Wes took out his water bottle and poured water over the metal surface. Jake rubbed off the silty mud with his shirt sleeve until he could read the words aloud: *"If you've found this, then more likely than not,*  *you've been followed. So, please heed my instructions."*

Wes gasped. "Whoa, how does this box know that someone is following us?"

Just then, a distant sound came from behind them—footfalls and muted voices. The kids looked at one another. Amber gulped, then whispered, "Sounds like they found us. And there's more than just one of them now."

Wes tapped the box with his finger. "Jake, hurry. Read the instructions."

Jake read them out loud.

1. The way out is up.
2. At the shelf, pull the keystone to force their path.
3. Climb fast.
4. They will come from the east. When they are below the eagle, you have 5 seconds to pull the lever.
5. Exit by stairs to the west.
6. Run.

They all looked up to where the crevice walls rose above them.

"Umm..." Wes took in a deep breath. "That's a *long* ways up."

"We can do it." Jake fixed his eyes on Wes. "We have to trust the instructions."

Amber was already feeling around the rock behind them. "Look over here," she said. Jake and Wes turned their headlamps around to find Amber already climbing. She reached up and slid her hand into a small but deep, notch in the granite wall. "It looks like someone carved holds into the rock." She continued to climb, and fast. Soon she was high above them. Jake put the metal box in his pack and followed her lead.

Before long, the handholds disappeared, but the crevice walls grew closer together.

"It's a chimney," Amber yelled down. "So you have to climb it like this." Amber pressed her hands and feet against the walls and climbed by carefully moving one foot on one side, and then the other across from it, then pressing her body upward a few inches at a time. "It's not that bad, and I can see a ledge. I think we can all fit on it."

Jake followed Amber, and Wes came up third. "Just don't look down. Just don't look down," Wes whispered to himself.

Amber made it to the ledge, then Jake. He looked down into the dark void where Wes was struggling against the walls of the chimney, his arms shaking.

"Give me your hand, Wes." Jake got on his knees and extended his arm down to him. "I'll help pull you up."

Wes shifted his weight to thrust his hand up to Jake— but his right foot slipped. Jake reached out and caught his hand just in time. But the force of Wes's fall threw Jake off balance, and he lurched forward over the edge. Amber grabbed Jake's collar and pulled him back.

After pulling Wes onto the ledge, Jake helped him to sit down. Wes heaved in deep breaths, and he looked to be close to tears. "You've got this, Wes" Jake bent down beside his cousin. "I know you can do it." Wes sniffled, wiped his nose on the sleeve of his shirt, and nodded.

Amber craned her neck, staring up into the crevice. "I think we're about halfway there. Jake, what are we supposed to do here? The instructions said to do something?"

"The instructions said, 'At the shelf, pull the keystone to force their path.'"

"Is this it?" Wes put his hands on a triangular-shaped stone fitted into a crack in the wall. He tugged on it, and it broke free. Immediately they could hear the sound of a rockfall. A massive plume of stone dust shot up from below them, rising through the air and blocking out the sunlight above.

"Whoa, that was cool!" Amber blinked her eyes in amazement. "I just hope we didn't crush those guys."

They waited and listened. The sound of angry voices and coughing soon came through the cloud of dust.

"It totally worked!" Wes blinked his eyes and shook his head. "Let's get this climbing over with, okay."

The voices of the men rose from the ground below. "The kids must've found it. We'll have to take it from them at the top."

Jake looked at Amber, both of their eyes wide. "Amber, can you keep leading us out?"

She nodded and squeezed her body up into the rock. "It's going to get tight up here," she called down, "but that makes it easier."

Jake wedged himself into the crack and continued the climb.

"Good thing I'm not claustrophobic—or acrophobic. That would be like a worst-case scenario," Wes muttered, "Oh, wait, I'm both of those."

"I know what claustrophobia is–" Jake pressed himself another foot up, "–but what's *acro*phobia?"

Wes coughed from the rising dust. "It's the fear of heights."

"You've got this, Wes." Amber kept climbing. "I'm almost there. At the top, we can help pull you up."

"Thanks," Wes called up, "but when we get to the top, I'm guessing we'll be standing on the head of these Owls, which is also not very comforting."

Amber squeezed her arms through the top and then pushed her hands against the sunlit rock until she could lean forward onto her belly. She slid her legs out from the crack and disappeared. Then Jake saw her hand reach down into the crevice. The sunlight blinded him as he pressed his head through the cramped opening at the top. He grabbed Amber's hand. A moment later, he stood at the top, dusting off his shorts. Then Wes's curly red hair appeared. Jake offered his hand and helped pull Wes to his feet.

Wes immediately sat down on the smooth granite and cradled his head in his hands. "This is exactly what I was afraid of. I feel dizzy."

They were standing on the granite head of one of the

Twin Owls. Jake peered over the edge and felt woozy. To
the west, he could see the flat blue-gray face of Longs
Peak, what people called "the diamond." A jagged set of
spires ran along its northern ridgeline, and clouds swirled
among the nearby peaks. He could see the town of Estes
Park, the white buildings of the Stanley Hotel, and the
rolling green meadows of old ranchlands. He turned to
the east, where the great wall of the Lumpy Ridge rose
from the meadows into the sky. That's when he saw
them: two men scrambling through the boulders, both
dressed more like they belonged at a business meeting
than on a hike in the mountains. Even from this
distance, Jake spotted the gray dust on their hair and
shoulders.

"They're coming! Look!" he pointed east, down into
the ravine.

Wes got up and edged his way over. He reached back
into the nape of his shirt and pulled out the compass that
hung around his neck. "Yep, it's just like the box said.
They're coming from the east."

"The instructions also said that the exit was to the
west." Amber started to explore the area behind them. "If
there's a way down, that means those guys can use it as a
way up. We're going to be totally trapped up here if we
don't get down and quick!"

She found the escape route and called the boys over. It

was a six-foot drop to a thin path. Then the path fell away into a steep ravine of scrubby trees and angular rock.

"That's the exit?" Wes exclaimed. "There is no way I'm going down that!"

"It's our only way off of this thing," Amber said.

"Wes, once we're on the path, it should be easy," Jake added. "We can lower you down first."

"You call that little piece of dirt and rocks a path?" Wes shook his head. Jake could see that he was trying to keep his cool, but his cousin was trembling. His hands shook. "Jake, I just can't do it."

"Wes, we've got no choice." Jake tried not to sound anxious, but he knew they didn't have much time. "The way we came up is blocked. And if we stay, they–" Jake pointed toward the ravine– "will eventually find the way up here."

"Oh, no!" Amber squeezed her eyes and furrowed her brow like she was straining to remember something important.

"What is it?" Jake asked.

"The instructions. They said we only have five seconds to do something, remember?"

"Shoot!" Wes clasped his hand over his mouth. "We totally forgot. It was something about an eagle and a lever."

Jake pulled the box out of his pack. "It says, '*When*

they are below the eagle, you have 5 seconds to pull the lever.'"
Jake glanced around. "I'll find the lever. You guys look for
the eagle."

Jake studied the cracks that ran along the crown of the
Owl. Nothing. He kept looking, but all he could see was
rock–nothing that looked even remotely like a lever.

"We found the eagle!" Wes yelled out.

Jake turned to see Wes pointing north across the curve
of the ravine. At the top of a polished cliff-face, wind and
water had sculpted the rock to resemble the regal head of a
bird.

"I can see the men, too." Amber shielded her eyes from
the sun. "They'll be right below the eagle soon."

"How much time do I have?" Jake asked.

"Maybe a couple of minutes." Wes had pulled out his
binoculars to get a better view. "They seem to be struggling. There's a lot of boulders and trees in their way, and
it looks super steep."

"Stay here, Wes," Amber said, "and let us know when
they get below the eagle. I'm going to help Jake." She ran
over to Jake who was now growing frantic searching for
the lever. "I bet it's somewhere along the edge. He
surveyed the rim but only saw the gray and pink rock.
"I'm going to lie on my belly and lean out to see if I can
find it."

"Be careful." She moved to his right. "I'll do the same

over here." They both wriggled out to the edge of the rock, looking for something that resembled a handle.

"They're getting closer!" Wes yelled. "You've got, like, *one* minute!"

Jake crept along the edge, moving toward Wes. "I think this is it!" Jake called to Amber.

She inched over to his side. Below them, just within arm's reach, was the top branch of a dead tree. At its base was a massive pile of logs.

"Okay, they're closing in." Wes followed the men with his binoculars. "You pull it when I say!" He started to countdown. "Ten, nine, eight, seven..."

Jake got his hand on the branch and readied his grip.

"...three, two, one—*pull*!"

Jake yanked on the branch as hard as he could.

Nothing happened.

"Amber, I need your help!"

She stretched but couldn't reach the lever.

"Guys, you have to pull, *now*!" Wes yelled.

He shouted so loud that the men below stopped for a moment and looked up, giving Jake and Amber two precious additional seconds.

She crawled closer, right up against Jake, stretched out her hand, and caught the branch. They both pulled with all their might until the lever snapped and fell from their grip.

"Oh no, we broke it! Jake rolled onto his back and started getting up.

When the branch snapped, the men raised their heads to see a long dark tree branch falling through the air. It bounced onto the rocks at the base of the dead tree, causing them to shift. With a loud crack, something released beneath the log pile. There was a rumble, followed by a groan. Then the logs broke free and tumbled down the cliffs, kicking up a rockslide as they fell.

The men turned around and clambered down the path as fast as they could, trying to escape from the logs and rocks that kept spilling down into the ravine. The debris began piling into a wall of stone and mangled wood that blocked their path.

Jake, Wes, and Amber burst into shouts of victory.

"You guys!" Wes was bouncing on his feet. "That was amazing! Can we do it again?"

"I think this only buys us enough time to get down." Jake put his hand on his cousin's shoulder. "Can you do it?"

Wes nodded. "I've got so much adrenaline in my body right now, I think I could jump down." He peered over the edge. "Okay, maybe not jump. Lower me down fast before this wears off and I have second thoughts."

Jake and Amber smiled. Wes lay down on the rock and let his feet dangle over the edge. The other two each grabbed one of his arms and carefully let him down until his feet touched the ground. Then Jake lowered Amber while Wes spotted. The two on the ground now supported Jake's feet and bolstered him as he slowly slid down the rock face.

"Whew." Jake let out a deep breath. "We made it!"

"And this trail isn't so bad once you get a bit further down." Wes gestured for them to follow him. "I think we can go fast. Remember the last instruction? It said: *run.*"

The three made their way down into the ravine on the west side of the Owls, found the faint trail they had taken earlier, and scrambled back to the main path. Then they sprinted all the way back to the trailhead.

"The bikes are still here!" Wes went to work on the combination.

"I bet they were so upset when the combination didn't work." Jake grinned.

Wes looked up from the lock. "Um, we've got a problem, guys. I forgot the new combination."

"Just think, Wes." Jake scanned the area for any sign of the two men.

Amber tried to help with the lock. "Did you put in your birthday or something like that?"

"It *was* something like that." Wes bit his lip and stared at the ground.

Jake continued watching the trail and scanning the woods.

"Got it!" Wes yelled. "It's eight-seven-eight-nine, the elevation of the Twin Owls!" He unraveled the lock from the bikes and threw it in his pack.

Amber and Jake ran over, and all three of them grabbed their bikes and pedaled away.

CHAPTER 21

1880

It was still dark as Abner led the way uphill through the forest. They followed a trail that long ago had been established by the Utes, or perhaps an ancient, now forgotten, tribe. The first several miles were easy going until Abner departed from the worn path to traverse a wooded ridge. Abe's job was to mark this new trail with ribbons of white cotton cloth. Every twenty to twenty-five steps, he would tie a strip to a tree branch to mark their route. They would come back later with axes and saws to clear the trees and deadfall that choked their path.

"Some folks from Denver want to climb the peak," Abner explained. "And I figure there's eventually going to be money in it. That's the future here, Abe: hospitality."

As they gained the crest of the ridge, the massive gray

face of Longs Peak came into view, close enough now to fill the sky.

"How do we get up it?" Abe tried to hide his fear from Abner, but the quaver in his voice gave him away.

"It gets a little tricky, about right there–" Abner pointed to a high point on the ridge "–but you're young and spry. You'll do just fine."

Abe took in a deep breath and stared up at the mountain again. It all felt impossible. *Impossible.* The force of that word stung. It was a word full of *nevers* and *nots*, of *ifs* and *don'ts*. It made him think of the city. *They said I'd never leave. That I couldn't save the money for the ticket. "Don't risk it." "It's not worth trying." Well, I'm here. They were wrong. And I guess this is what being free looks like. Like risk. Like trust.*

They pressed forward, the forest giving way to rock and tundra. Soon, the tundra disappeared, too, and they entered an enormous boulder field. Ghostly streams of mist flowed down the mountainside and gathered around them. Somehow, Abner knew the way through the fog, and they made their way to the foot of a long incline of pink and orange granite.

"This way, Abe." Abner pointed up the incline.

Abe needed to use his hands to crawl up the long, stone ramp. The incline eventually leveled off, and he could see their next waypoint, a gap between two giant, jagged stone teeth. They scrambled through the window, across a series of exposed ledges, and then up through a narrow channel in the rock. Abe's hands were shaking now, partly from fatigue but also from fear. The rock wall was almost vertical.

"Here's our homestretch, Abe," Abner called back.

"Mr. Sprague, I don't know if I can do this." Abe's voice was shaky. "What if I just stay on the ledge below, and you go up?"

"You can do this, kid. Just put one hand in front of the other, and keep your fingers in the cracks. They'll hold ya."

"Okay," Abe replied, his voice hesitant.

"And don't look back," Abner added. "That'd be a bad idea."

The wind whipped around them as they climbed. Hand over hand, step by step, they made their way closer to the top. Then Abner disappeared over the edge. Moments later, his hand stretched out to help Abe.

They stood on the summit, a broad space riddled with boulders. Abe was speechless. The Rocky Mountains below stretched for hundreds of miles to the north and the south. To the west, more mountains. In the east, the sun was still rising over the prairies. The world here was somehow familiar, like he had once seen it in a dream. He took it all in. Not wanting to forget the sight, he pulled out his journal and made a hurried sketch of the panorama.

"Hank March says that the Arapahoe would come up here for eagle feathers." Abner walked over to a depression in the rock. "Warriors would hide in a hole like this one, between the rocks, holding a coyote pelt over them. When the eagle fell upon the hide, the warrior grabbed the bird by its feet."

"That would take some patience," Abe remarked.

"Anything worthwhile does," Abner replied.

Abe soon learned that going down the mountain was much more daunting than going up. Instead of feeling his way forward with his fingers, he had to find his way down with the leather tip of his boots. He was relieved when they finally arrived at the boulder field, where the terrain felt stable and flat compared to the stone walls they had scrambled up while climbing to the top. Back in the forest, they found the white strips of cloth hanging in the trees.

"You marked the way–" Abner gestured toward the woods– "so how about you lead us back."

Abe moved to the front and followed the white strips

of cloth until a hand fell on his shoulder. He turned to see Abner with a finger to his lips. "Stay still," Abner whispered.

A soft crunch of pine needles came from somewhere on their right. By instinct, they both crouched low to the ground.

"Abner Sprague," a gruff voice called from the mist, "you sound like a moose in rut crashing through this forest."

Abner stood upright as a figure materialized before them, a man so full of beard it was impossible to tell his age. He was covered from head to toe in dark buckskin that had been coated in bear grease and beeswax. A curved nose poked out from the beard along with two piercing green eyes.

"Hank March!" Abner jumped to his feet and embraced the mountain man. "What brings you back into the valley?"

"How about a dinner at your place?" March said. "I've got a brace of fresh grouse in my pack that should feed the three of us." He offered his hand to Abe. "Hank March. Pleasure to meet ya, young man."

Abe shook the man's hand. "Abe, sir. It's a pleasure to meet you, too."

"That wasn't a proper introduction, young man." Hank looked at Abe askance. "What's your last name?"

"He ain't got one," Abner answered.

"You sure he ain't Jesse James trying to hide his identity?" March gave Abner a stern look, then smiled.

"Hank, you know James is 'round thirty-five. Least that's what the papers say. This young man is half that."

"I'm just poking at ya, Abe." Hank smiled and winked. "Don't mind me none. You got a good honest look about ya—" he patted his own chest– "and I'm an excellent judge of character."

The two men and Abe walked and talked their way down from the mountain and into the valley. By the time they reached the ranch, the sun had set, and the cattle had gathered close to the barns. Abe knew that this was his chance. Perhaps Hank March could explain the mysterious markings of the spearhead.

CHAPTER 22

THE DISCOVERY

An hour later, after taking backroads into town, Jake, Amber, and Wes coasted into the Moraine Park Campground. Mrs. Catalina was sitting outside by herself, reading a book.

"Hi, Mom," Amber called out as she jumped off her bike and walked it into the gravel drive of the campsite.

Mrs. Catalina looked up from her book. "Welcome back." She was surprised to see dirt and dust clinging to the kids' clothes. A cobweb had wrapped itself across Wes's hair. "Wow! You three are in need of some showers."

Amber looked down at her dirt-stained shirt and scuffed knees. "I think we could use some food first." She glanced around the campsite. "Where is everyone?"

"They're still on their hike up to Timberline Falls. They should be back in a couple hours, and we'll go for a proper meal then. You three can grab some snacks out of our fridge if you want."

"I'll get some chips from our camper." Jake parked his bike beside Amber's and went inside to rummage through the cupboards.

Wes laid his bike down in the gravel and trudged over to the picnic table. "I'm going to sit over here and defend the table from the squirrels." He plopped down, put his head on the table, and let out a long sigh.

Amber and Jake returned with food and drinks and sat down across from Wes. Jake unzipped his backpack and pulled out the metal box. "Wes, can I borrow your knife?"

"Sure." Wes unsnapped the holster on his belt, took out the Swiss army knife, and handed it to his cousin. "You know, Jake, you've really got to get a knife of your own. Especially if you're going to keep leading us on dangerous missions."

"You're right." Jake pulled out the flathead screwdriver tool on the knife. "I brought some allowance money with me. Maybe I can pick one up at the gift shop before we leave." He slid the screwdriver under the lid of the metal box, gently using it as a lever to pry it open. It wouldn't budge. He removed the screwdriver from the front edge of the box and moved it to the right side, but the lid remained stuck. When he tried the left side, the metal creaked, then snapped. He had broken the seal of rust that had kept the lid frozen in place. Jake grabbed it with his hand and pried it open. As he did, Amber and Wes leaned in to get a better look.

Inside lay a small, weathered leather journal. Jake lifted it out of the box. Its color had faded, leaving only a hint of red. Afraid it might fall apart in his hands, he opened it carefully. When he did, a small piece of paper fell out of the journal and onto the table.

"What's that?" Amber tapped on the table beside the paper.

Jake picked it up and squinted as he studied it. "It's a train ticket." He read the printing on it out loud: "*Philadelphia to Denver, May 14th, 1880.*"

Wes leaned in further, his nose almost touching the ticket. After looking at the words quietly, he sat back, and repeated out loud, "Eighteen-eighty." He paused. "So, this journal has got to be at least one hundred and forty years old!"

"It must be," Jake said in a hushed tone. The little book in his hands was heavy and dense, like a thousand mysteries might be contained inside. He gently turned one of the yellowed pages to reveal a drawing.

"What is *that* thing?" Amber leaned on her elbows to get closer to Jake and the journal.

"It looks like a sketch of an...um...an...arrowhead," Jake said, then bit his lip. "I guess it is, but it's got weird symbols and stuff drawn all over it." He turned to the next page to reveal another drawing. "And this one looks almost the same, but the markings are different."

"Look, it's got a note scribbled underneath it." Wes reached out and set his finger on the page, where a faded set of letters were scribbled underneath the drawing.

Jake pulled the journal closer to his eyes and read the words. It says... He squinted to make out the writing. "Silver Spearhead. Found at Dunraven Ranch, May 1880."

Silver Spearhead. Found at Dunraven Ranch, May 1880

"What I want to know–" Wes scratched the side of his face–"is why somebody would need to hide it the way they did? If a big piece of silver were in that metal box, it would make sense. But these are just a couple drawings."

"*And*, why were those two guys after it?" Amber added.

"Whoever hid it–" Jake gently laid the journal on the table and picked up the metal box, "–somehow knew the wrong people would be coming after it." He turned it over and read from the words scratched into its rusty surface: "*If you've found this, then more likely than not, you've been followed. So, please heed my instructions.*"

Wes shrugged. "I don't know how to explain that one. But whoever hid that journal knew it was valuable–valuable enough that they were trying to keep it from..." As Wes paused, Jake finished his thought, "Probably from the same people who Mather tried to warn me about."

"So, do you think that your grandpa is the one who hid it in the crevice?" Amber asked.

"I thought about that almost the entire bike ride back here." Jake furrowed his brow and set the box back on the table. "Remember the note inside the package from Mather? Where he said, 'All we have learned has been entrusted to the Marmot'?"

Wes and Amber nodded, then his finger shot out

toward Jake. "And we discovered that your *grandpa* is *the Marmot*."

"So, what if this scavenger hunt wasn't my grandpa's idea?"

Wes and Amber looked confused, so Jake hurried to explain. "What I mean is, my grandpa's friends–the ones who were in the radio club with him–what if *they* were on a scavenger hunt?"

Wes closed his eyes and seemed to be concentrating on Jake's last words. Suddenly, his eyes shot open. "You mean a *treasure* hunt."

Jake nodded slowly. "Jasper gave me the package just when I was leaving the cabin, and he said something to me that I keep replaying in my head."

"What was it?" Amber asked.

"'*We* trust you.'" Jake paused for a second, thinking. "Jasper didn't say, 'I trust you." He said, '*We* trust you.'"

Jake picked the journal up again and worked his way through the pages. "There's nothing else in it, just the drawings." He turned to the very front and saw something that made his jaw drop. After a moment, he looked up at his friends, eyes wide. "You're not going to believe this."

"Well, tell us," Wes replied.

Jake read the entry aloud: "This journal is the property of Abraham Longsight Evans."

"That's so cool," Wes said. "It belonged to a guy who had the same last name as you."

Jake sat in stunned silence, still staring at the page. Wes and Amber waited for him to say something.

"I'll be right back." Jake got up and ran to his camper. A moment later, he returned with the scrapbook and began flipping wildly through its pages. "This is it." He pointed to a black and white photograph where an older man stood with his arm around a teenage boy, a long white banner fluttered in the breeze behind them. "It's from the 1915 dedication of Rocky Mountain National Park. My dad said that this kid..."

"Whoa!" Wes looked at Jake and back at the picture. "That kid looks *just* like you!"

"Yeah, my dad said that he's my great-great-grandfather." Jake pulled the photo out of its mounts and flipped it over.

All three sat up and read the writing on the back, their mouths agape.

In a fine ink script, was written:

Jacob Ulysses Evans (Age 15), Abraham Longsight Evans (Age 52).

CHAPTER 23

LEAVING

That night, Jake joined Wes in his tent. The boys were wrapped up in their sleeping bags, looking through the mesh ceiling at a dark sky full of stars.

"Jake?" Wes's voice was sleepy, tired from a day full of adventure.

"Yeah?"

"Thanks for including me." Wes paused, and Jake wasn't sure how to respond. Wes cleared his throat. "I could tell that you wanted to keep the scrapbook...and scavenger hunt and stuff more...I guess...private. I'm just glad that you changed your mind and let me and Amber be part of it."

Jake gazed at the treetops. The long pine needles appeared to dance in the soft light of the fading campfire.

"Yeah... I'm glad, too. At first, I thought that keeping it all a secret would keep it...you know...special."

"But instead, you did exactly what your grandpa told you to do."

Jake rubbed his forehead, trying to figure out what Wes meant. "Um...I don't think I understand. What did my grandpa say?"

"In the cipher." Wes turned away from the stars to face Jake. "Remember? He said: *Seek help early. Learn from friends.*"

The words made Jake chuckle. "I guess I was so excited about figuring out the cipher that I didn't think about the words. How did you remember that anyway?"

Wes tapped his forehead. "I told you, Jake; I remember the weirdest stuff."

Jake smiled. "And you *forget* stuff, too–like your bike combination."

Wes swung his arm around and gave Jake a playful jab to his belly. They both laughed.

"I remember the next part, too: *Every real treasure exploits neglect.* I've been thinking about it." Wes gazed back up at the stars. "I think it means that people...they overlook stuff. They forget what the real treasures are."

"Do *you* think there's a real treasure?" Jake asked. "That there's something my grandpa and his friends were trying to find."

Wes was quiet for such a long time that Jake began to wonder if he'd fallen asleep. "Yeah, I do think there's a treasure. I've got no idea what it is, but I think it's for real."

"I do, too." Jake pulled his sleeping bag up around his chin.

Wes sighed again. "Jake, my brain feels kinda scrambled."

"Scrambled?"

"Yeah. I've been going through all the clues in my head, trying to put them together. First, we followed the morse code in the scrapbook to Emerald Lake, and we found that old bottle. The clue in the bottle led us to the Apache Fort, where we discovered the location of the cabin along Fall River Road. Then, you figured out how that weird old sculpture thingy pointed to Twin Owls. We went there and found the metal box with the journal in it. Which belonged to your great-grandpa."

"My great-great-grandpa. There's two 'greats.'"

"That's too many 'greats' for me to remember."

"Let's just call him my *Grandpa Abe*. That'll make it easy."

Wes nodded. "Good idea." He paused. "There's just so many clues. I mean, how do we know the journal was the thing your grandpa wanted you to find?"

Jake thought for a moment. "Well, I've checked the scrapbook, and there's no more clues for this park. And the journal has all kinds of notes and drawings in it, but nothing that looks like it might be the next clue. That makes me think the journal is what we were supposed to find."

"How about the box?" Wes asked.

"The metal thing we found at Twin Owls?"

"No, the one that old ranger, Jasper, gave you."

"I've been wondering about that, too."

Wes shrugged his shoulders. "We could just break it open."

Jake shook his head. "We can't damage it."

"Why not? I mean, it's *yours* now."

"I'm the *keeper*, not the *owner*." Jake checked the zipper on his sleeping bag and secured the velcro strap to keep it in place. "It makes me think about when I was a little kid and my brother, Nick, let me fly his drone. It was fun–until I crashed it into a tree and broke it. Nick was nice about it and all, but I felt awful. It was special, and it wasn't mine. I feel the same way about that box."

"My dad always says, 'Wes, trust your gut.' I bet this is something like that, where you should just trust your gut."

Jake nodded in the dark and yawned.

Then Wes yawned and attempted to talk at the same time. "You know...yawns are...contagious...even in...the dark." He rolled onto his side and pulled the sleeping bag over his shoulders. "I think I'm starting to fall asleep."

"Me, too." Jake fluffed his pillow and nestled his head back into its soft flannel case.

"So, how do we find the next clue?"

"I guess the scrapbook," Jake said. "Our next park is the Great Sand Dunes, so we should look through the pages that have pictures of the dunes."

Wes mumbled something Jake couldn't understand.

"What did you say, Wes?"

Wes didn't respond. He'd fallen asleep.

In the morning, the three families tore down camp and packed up their things. After helping Wes with his tent, Jake stood at the edge of the campsite and looked out over Moraine Park. He tried to soak in the vision of the place. Rocky Mountain National Park had left a mark on his heart, an impression that would stay with him for the rest of his life. As he watched the leaves flutter on distant aspen trees, he made a promise to himself. He would return. One day, he would come back to discover its other secrets: the park's many waterfalls and summits, its alpine lakes and hidden streams, and the stories it had yet to tell. His heart felt like it was growing in his chest, expanding so that it could somehow absorb the splendor of the sunrise on the mountains. *This must be what Grandpa felt.*

A warm hand gently grabbed his shoulder. "You sure are deep in thought," his dad said. "What are you thinking about?"

Jake took in a breath and let out a long, satisfying sigh. "About this place and how Grandpa must have felt about it."

Jake's dad pulled him close, and they both gazed out at the meadow as the first soft rays of pink sunlight colored the steam rising from the creek. "*This* is what he wanted, Jake. He hoped that you would fall in love with this place—just like he did." His dad smiled. "I can see it in your eyes. They glimmer like your grandpa's did when he discovered a new place."

Down the hill from the campground, a white truck made its way along Cub Lake Road and then parked in a gravel pullout beside the meadow. The door opened, and a young ranger with blond, braided hair stepped out. She held a set of binoculars to her eyes. Then she pulled out a small book from her backpack and jotted down some notes.

"Hey, Dad, that's Ranger Ellie. I'm going to go say goodbye to her."

His dad smiled and gently slapped Jake on the back. "Okay, but be quick. We're leaving soon."

Jake ran down the steep hillside and crossed the road. Ellie startled at the sound of Jake's feet on the gravel beside her. "Oh, I'm sorry," Jake said. "I didn't mean to surprise you."

"Well, this is a *great* surprise." She smiled; let go of the binoculars, allowing them to hang around her neck; and set her hands on her hips.

"What are you up to?" Jake asked.

"Counting the elk calves." She pointed out a pair of cows snuggled up with their white-spotted babies. "Those two over there are new, born sometime in the last couple of days."

Jake watched as one of the mothers nosed her calf. The baby stood up, its legs quivering, and took a few wobbly steps. "That's incredible."

"It sure is," Ellie said. She turned back to Jake. "So, tell me. Did you find what you were looking for?"

A big grin spread across his face. "I sure did." Jake wished that he had time to recount the story of the last few days.

"Where are you headed next?" she asked.

"The Great Sand Dunes."

Her eyes lit up. "You're going to *love* it there. In fact, I've heard that the mountains near the dunes got loads of snow this year. So, Medano Creek–the creek that flows through the dunes—is flowing faster than it has in over a century."

"Wow, that sounds really cool."

Just then, someone called his name from the campground. He turned to see his mom waving for him to return.

"Well, I guess we're leaving. I wanted to say thanks for helping me out and for the map."

She reached out her hand. "You're welcome, Jake Evans."

He shook her hand.

"Goodbye, Ellie." Jake turned and ran back up the hill.

Wes was waiting for him, his curly red hair still tousled from sleep. He was studying a guidebook as he walked. "Hey Jake, guess what? You won't believe this!" Wes looked over his shoulder. "Amber! Come here. You've got to see this!"

She was talking with her dad. "Just a minute!" she called back. Jake noticed that Mr. Catalina had handed her something.

Amber ran to join them. "Hey, this is for you." She

gave Jake an envelope. "My dad said the campground attendant came by and dropped it off." Jake looked over the envelope addressed to him with a printed label.

Amber rubbed her shoulders to warm them up, then pressed her hands into the back pockets of her jeans. She looked at Wes. "What did you want to show us?"

Jake began to tear the edge of the envelope.

"Jake." Wes elbowed him in the side. "Check this out." He pointed at a page in the guidebook.

Jake folded the envelope, slid it into his back pocket, and looked at the page Wes was trying to show them.

"You can *sandboard* at the Great Sand Dunes!" Wes said. "Like snowboarding, but on the *sand*!"

"That sounds awesome!" Amber said, as she and Jake studied the pictures of the sand dunes in Wes's book.

Wes closed the book. "Do you guys know where we're stopping for lunch?"

"How can you be hungry?" Amber replied. "We just had breakfast."

Wes groaned. "I'm growing, I guess–at least I hope I am. I'm tired of being so short."

"My dad said we're stopping in Buena Vista." Jake pronounced it: *Boo-na Vee-sta*. "It's like four hours from here."

Amber laughed and corrected his pronunciation.

"*Beautiful view*–that's what *Buena Vista* means in Spanish."

Uncle Brian's voice broke up their conversation. "Let's load up!"

"Okay, I guess I'll see you guys in a few hours." Jake turned to take one last look at the mountains. The RV's big motor started, followed by the familiar thrum of his parents' truck. He ran over and got in.

As they pulled out of the campground, Jake studied the envelope. The front was postmarked September 15th, 2018, and a yellow sticker on the front read: *Deliver on June 2nd, 2019.* He tore open the envelope and pulled out a note written in his grandpa's handwriting. Jake could feel the buzz of excitement in his chest. His shoulders lifted, and he took in a deep breath when he saw the first word, *Jax,* the nickname his grandpa had given to him.

Jax,

When I was a young man, I received a letter–like the one you are holding now–from my grandfather, Abraham Longsight Evans. It contained a list of things he wanted to give to me in his will. The list was short–just two items: a scrapbook and a journal. The letter ended with the words, "Find my journal, and keep it hidden."

When he died, the estate was settled, and I was

given the scrapbook—but no journal. I searched through his belongings to no avail. I asked my dad and my Aunt Margie, but they had never seen a journal. About two years passed, and one day, while flipping through the scrapbook, I began to discover clues hidden away within its pages. They led me into the national parks. And in those parks, I stumbled upon more clues: hidden drawings on rocks in Arizona, numbers carved into trees in Washington, a buried message in an old tobacco tin in California. The signs and hints were like dots on a connect-the-dots page. Every time I explored a new park, more dots appeared. I started to see patterns, and a picture began to emerge.

I met friends along the way, including Jasper and Mather. And like my grandfather, I concealed all we've learned within the pages of the scrapbook. I never found the journal, but my friends and I came to believe it was hidden somewhere in Rocky Mountain National Park.

When I was diagnosed with cancer, I realized that it was my time—not to give up—but to pass the quest on to someone I love and trust. That person is you, Jax.

I hope you've found the journal by now. However, if you haven't, you've got plenty of time—an entire lifetime—to return and search for it. If you did find it, be sure to keep it hidden. We' ve reason to believe that it's valuable and that there are others looking for it—people who cannot be trusted. This quest, I suppose, is much bigger than either you or I understand.

Your next clue:
Click, Click, Click, Click, Click, Click.
They become visible in the dark.
Assemble the vista,
And look for the mark.

With Deep Affection,
Grandpa (The Marmot)

PS: I assume you've met Jasper, and he's given you the box. Keep it locked. You'll find the key in due time.

Chapter 24

1880

After dinner, Abe joined Hank and Abner in the rocking chairs set around the stone fireplace of Abner's cabin. "Mr. March, sir, I was hoping you could help me with something."

"Well, Abe, whatcha got on your mind?"

Abe pulled the leather-bound journal from his back pocket, opened it to his drawings of the spearhead, and handed it to Hank. The mountain man stared at the pages in the flicker of the firelight. He mumbled something to himself and then gave the journal back to Abe. Leaning back in his chair, Hank placed his hands behind his head and closed his eyes. Abe waited and watched as the grizzled man appeared to have fallen asleep. But his lips moved like he was talking to someone in a dream. Then his eyes flashed open. Hank leaned forward in his chair towards Abe. "Tell me: what happened to the silver object?"

Stunned, Abe looked down at his drawings and then back to Hank's serious face. The orange flames of the fire reflected in his eyes. "How did you know it was made of silver?"

"I'll tell ya." Hank pinched his scruffy bottom lip. "But first, you tell me what's become of it."

"We returned the spearhead," Abe replied. "It belongs to a widow in town who said she found it along the old Ute trail."

Hank sighed with relief, but concern was still evident in the creases around his eyes and mouth. He turned to Abner. "Does anyone else know about this?"

Abner rocked back and forth slowly in his chair. He had pulled out a pouch of tobacco and was stuffing the sweet-smelling leaves into the bowl of his pipe. "Yes. Most of the ranch hands know about it. Folks in town have been talking. And Dunraven."

Hank's jaw tightened at the mention of the rancher's name.

Abner continued. "It appears that his foreman, Ted Whyte, somehow got his hands on it. I surmise by illegitimate means. Abe here came upon Whyte and his crew attemptin' to bury it somewhere on Dunraven's ranch."

Hank, his bushy eyebrows raised in surprise, turned to Abe.

"Bad timing, I guess." Abe rubbed the back of his neck. "They caught me and locked me up. Of course, I got away. Then I dug up the thing and brought it here."

Hank scratched his beard where it grew thick along his chin. "Then you returned it to the woman in town?"

Abner nodded. "I had one of the boys deliver it to Mrs. Cartwright." Abner struck a match and lit his pipe. He offered the pouch to Hank, who took it and withdrew a pipe from the inside pocket of his buckskin jacket.

"I've got a bad feeling, Abner. About Dunraven being involved."

"Mr. March..." Abe began.

Hank cleared his throat. "I know, kid. You're wonderin' how I knew the thing was made of silver." He lit his pipe. Abe could hear the leaves sizzle. "What I'm going to tell you both, you got to swear to keep between us."

Abe and Abner both nodded.

"In all my wanderin' and trappin', I've been fortunate enough to be counted a friend among many of the native peoples. They all have their tales. But there's one old story I've heard a handful of times. And by 'old,' I mean *real old*. It's been passed down from what some call 'the ancient ones.' Further south, I've heard 'em referred to as the Anasazi: a people who vanished from the earth."

Abe's imagination had been captured. He rested his elbows on his knees, cradled his chin in his hands, and listened.

"It's told with different details, but every version of the story tells of two silver spearheads." Hank paused to take a draw from his pipe. "Like I said, there were two of 'em. One of the spearheads they call *The Key*, and the other was named *Spinning Star*. As the story goes, the objects were fashioned of moonlight, liquid silver that fell from the sky as shooting stars. A young warrior–one of these *ancient ones*–was on a vision quest when he saw the stars streak across the night sky. He followed their path and found them in the dirt, still pulsing with the light of the moon. He took them and became their keeper. The warrior then wandered the land for nearly a hundred years. And into the silver surface of the spearheads, he carved something more valuable than the silver itself."

Abe inhaled a deep breath, as if he was trying to take in the mystery of what he was hearing.

Hank rested the pipe on his knee. "As some tell it, *The Key* unlocks a treasure, something the warrior found and hid deep in the earth. Other versions of the story say that he discovered a great river of silver flowing inside the mountains. And whoever has the spearheads can use them to find the treasure, or the river, or whatever it is the warrior discovered.

"Some versions of the story say that the warrior separated *the Key* from the *Spinning Star*, hiding *the Key* somewhere in the north and t*he Spinning Star* in the south."

Abner stood up, placed two thick logs on the fire, and then turned around to warm his backside. "So, you're afraid that Dunraven will get his hands on it again and find the treasure?"

Hank grimaced. "First off, Hank March ain't *afraid* of nothin'. However, you could rightly say that I am *concerned.*"

The faintest curve of a smile lifted Abner's lips. "I stand corrected, Hank."

"No offense taken, friend." He smiled at Abner, and the tight lines of worry on his face softened. Hank paused in thought for a moment, and the concerned look returned. "It ain't just him, though. It's folks like Dunraven." Abe could feel a note of anger in Hank's voice. "Men are moving in from the East, men who don't care 'bout the land. They've only got a mind for what they can take out of it. Going about digging holes in the earth, killin' all the deer and the elk. And when they've drained all the good out of a place, they move on to the next spot to do the same."

Abe's thoughts went back to the city. To the factory

and the kids who had worked beside him. He remembered the acrid smell of chemicals, iron, and burning coal. He could see the river through the dirty factory windows, one that had once flowed clear, now murky and clogged with debris.

"If there really is a treasure—" Hank's jaw stiffened—"those Dunraven-types will use it to buy up, control, and ruin everything."

Hank went silent. Abner picked up a metal poker leaning against the fireplace, moved the logs around in the fire, and sat back down. "Hank, I sense that there's more you want to tell us."

Hank nodded. "I do. Not three months back, I come out of the woods and into the town of Bozeman to get supplies. Two men, well-dressed and armed, came lookin' for me. Said they were employed by some company associated with the railroad and were doing what they called 'intelligence gatherin'.' These two fellers got wind that I'd traveled most of the country between Bozeman and Sante Fe, and heard that I was on friendly terms with a number of the tribes. So, they asked me if I ever seen or heard anythin' about a big arrowhead made of silver. Of course, I lied to 'em." Hank laughed to himself. "Then they give me this calling card—" he reached into the breast pocket of his jacket, pulled out a small card, and handed it to Abe— "and they said that if I heard anythin', to contact their employer."

Abe read the card: *Stanley Ferguson. Yellowstone National Park Improvement Company.*

Stanley Ferguson.
Yellowstone National Park
Improvement Company

He handed it back to Hank, who threw the card into the fire, where it curled and quickly turned to ash.

Hank leaned back in his chair. "I asked around about this Ferguson character. Guess he's one of those Easterners trying to gather up investors. Mining down south. Railroad work up north. He's got more irons in more fires than he knows what to do with.

"You know how it works, Abner. It's a big land out here, but word travels fast. And the folks in town who know about Mrs. Cartwright's silver object–they're going to talk. And that talk is going to work its way up to Bozeman–if it hasn't already–and eventually to this Ferguson feller."

Abe felt a stirring in his belly, like fear and excitement swirling around together. He stared into the glowing embers of the fire, and he could feel his heartbeat slow. It became stronger, like it was trying to match its beating to the rhythm of a distant drum. Hank's next words came from that same far-off place, somewhere over mountains and rolling plains–beyond time itself. "Abe, I've got a sense that you happened upon that silver spearhead for a reason." Hank's eyes glimmered in the firelight. "Might be happenstance. Might even be providence. But my gut says that you've got a part to play in all this."

Abe's mind took him back to the summit of Longs Peak, the cold wind in his face and hundreds of miles of country stretched out below him. He felt a calling. A responsibility.

He looked at Abner, then to Hank. "I don't know what you've got in mind, but I'll do it."

THE END

The story continues in book two:
Discovery in Great Sand Dunes National Park
See the preview chapter at the end of this book.

Author's Notes

This book includes real places and some references to historical figures. I figured that many of my readers might be curious about these, so I decided to include some additional details and author notes. You'll also find some links to products, like maps and hiking gear. Some of these are affiliate links. That means, when you purchase something from one of these links, the author makes a small commission from your purchase (another great way to support this book series).

Dunraven and Theodore Whyte: These guys were real characters living in the Estes Valley in the late 1800s. There's a trailhead and a mountain on the north end of Rocky Mountain national park named after Dunraven. Originally from England, he traveled the United States to hunt wild game. One of his trips was even guided by the famous Buffalo Bill Cody. Dunraven and Whyte decided to buy up the Estes Park valley and turn it into a private game reserve for wealthy clients. They used questionable tactics to obtain land from settlers and eventually had to sell the land and leave town.

Abner Sprague and his brother settled in Moraine Park and built a ranch and lodge. He and Dunraven had some real altercations. On one occasion, Whyte and two other cowboys ordered Sprague off of his land. When he didn't listen, they purposefully ran two-hundred head of cattle onto Sprague's ranch. To keep the cattle there, they put down salt. But Sprague had a cattle dog, who quickly chased the cows back toward town. The cow ran so fast that they beat Whyte and his cowboys back into Estes Park. Whyte tried this a second time, and Sprague returned the cattle in the same way, then had a heated confrontation with the cattleman. Sprague later moved to Glacier Basin, where he built a lodge and dammed a creek to create what is today known as Sprague Lake. The short hike around the lake makes for a perfect place to enjoy a sunset in Rocky Mountain National Park. You can find more history and information about Sprague and Dunraven on the National Parks Website: https://www.nps.gov/parkhistory/online_books/romo/buchholtz/chap4.htm

Moraine Park is one of the most beautiful and accessible places to visit in Rocky Mountain National Park. I highly recommend the campground at Moraine Park, especially the campsites along the south end of the campground that offer great views of the valley and the Big Thompson River.

Maps: If your family is hiking or camping, I highly recommend National Geographic Trails Illustrated maps https://amzn.to/35cDorI

Backcountry Camping and Wilderness Permits: There are campsites that you can hike to deeper within the park. In the story, Jake visits the Wilderness Office, where he meets Jasper and receives the package. This is often a busy place where you can plan out a backpacking trip with the help of a ranger and reserve the campsites for your trip. Get more information at: https://www.nps.-gov/romo/planyourvisit/wilderness-camping.htm

Four Lakes and a Waterfall Hike: In the story, Jake, Amber, and Wes hike a big loop that takes them to Bear Lake, Lake Haiyaha, Dream Lake, and Nymph Lake. Along the way, they stop to take in the most popular waterfall in the park, Alberta Falls. This 6.4-mile hike is strenuous, especially for those visiting from lower altitudes, but a wonderful way to see a lot of the park in a short time. In chapter eleven, they add a segment to Emerald Lake. If you're visiting RMNP, the hike from Bear Lake to Emerald is one of the best short hikes in the park. You can learn more at my hiking website:

- https://dayhikesneardenver.com/4-lakes-and-waterfall-loop-rocky-mountain-national-park/
- https://dayhikesneardenver.com/emerald-lake-hike-rocky-mountain-national-park/

Would you let your kids hike alone, like the kids do in the book? To be honest, I wouldn't allow them to hike without adult supervision until they were older teenagers. And I wouldn't ever be comfortable with them hiking solo. There's safety in groups, and most backcountry injuries and deaths occur when people are hiking alone. When we hike as a family, we always stay within eyesight of one another. I think that's a good principle. (Though, I'll admit that it would make for a really boring story).

Does it really snow in the summer in Colorado? We get a lot of snow in the mountains in the Spring and sometimes in early Summer. It can be deceptive if you're staying in Denver, where it's sunny and eighty degrees, because when you drive up into the mountains, the temperature drops, and the weather can be completely different. This is another reason why it's important to always pack the Ten Essentials.

The Ten Essentials: Dayhikers tend to get into more problematic situations than multi-day backpackers. When you think about it, it makes a lot of sense. Backpackers tend to do more planning, and they pack their packs with all kinds of stuff, including food and multiple sets of clothing. I advise that you make a habit of always carrying the Ten Essentials with you, even on short one-hour hikes. You can learn more about the Ten Essentials and purchase the items you need at REI.com.

Waterfalls in Rocky Mountain National Park: There are so many waterfalls in Rocky Mountain National Park. For more information on waterfall hikes, check out our 10 Waterfalls in RMNP page: https://dayhikesnear-denver.com/10-waterfall-hikes-rocky-mountain-national-park/

The Apache Fort is a real place but not a popular destination. I read about it in an old book and went to Rocky Mountain National Park to scout the location for this book. At the visitor center, I asked a group of Rangers about it, and all three of them had never heard of the place–but they were very interested. We found it the same way that Jake, Amber, and Wes discovered it, near a spring along the old Ute Trail. The drawing of the springhouse is real, and so is the writing on the rocks of the Apache Fort. I added the latitude and longitude coordinates, but the writing on the rock appears to have been painted by USGS (United States Geological Survey) workers many decades ago and most likely notes the location of the Apache Fort.

Fall River Road is another one of my favorite places

in the park, and just like in the story, it's closed for much of the year and a great place for a long bicycle ride. For vehicles, the traffic is one-way from the bottom to the top. At the top, you can visit the Alpine Visitor Center and watch the fog and clouds flow past. If you decide to hike or bike in this area, be alert for weather conditions and lightning. After driving to the top, you can drive down Trail Ridge Road back into Estes Park or head west to Grand Lake.

The Willow Park cabin was built in 1923 for the maintenance workers taking care of Fall River Road. The **Old Man of the Mountain sculpture** is based on a real sculpture that at one time was on the mantle in the mess hall of a local camp. A camp counselor working at the camp found a gnarled tree root and carved it into the shape of an old man hiking with a staff. That camp counselor grew up to become a famous American artist, Grant Wood, the painter of American Gothic. I've tried to find out what happened to the sculpture but have yet to solve that mystery.

The Twin Owls is a popular climbing destination in Rocky Mountain National Park, but I made up the crevice inside of it for the story. It likely has some crevices, but none as deep into the heart of the owls as the one Jake, Amber, and Wes discover. Getting to the top of the Twin Owls requires professional climbing services and gear.

Longs Peak is the centerpiece of Rocky Mountain National Park. It's climbed every year by thousands of people, and that heavy traffic can be part of what makes the climb dangerous. Abner Sprague did climb Longs Peak, and in the 1870s, people like Reverand Elkanah Lamb and his son Carlyle began guiding tourists up the mountain. Sprague made his final ascent to the top of Longs Peak when he was 74-years old. While Jake and his friends could not climb it, I wanted to give my readers the experience of Abe climbing to the top.

"It all turns on affection." The quote at the beginning of this book comes from two places. I've attributed it to Wendell Berry because it's the title and the central idea of a talk he gave in 2012. He was actually quoting from E.M. Forester's book, *Howard's End.* The idea is similar to Jesus' words: "For where your treasure is, there your heart will be also" (Matthew 6:21). Our affection for places: our homes, towns, schools, places of worship, local and national parks, all fire our imaginations with ways to preserve and care for them. It's the opposite of using. It's loving. If you would like to read his talk, you can find it here: https://www.neh.gov/about/awards/jefferson-lecture/wendell-e-berry-biography

About the Author

As I've hiked throughout different national parks and my home of Colorado, I've imagined stories about young boys and girls searching for treasure and, in the process, discovering the best treasure of all: the beauty of wild places. I've been inspired by my own searches for a treasure in the gorges and caves of Ohio, and by my dad, who discovered an ancient Native American settlement when he was just a teenager.

I've spent about six months of my life guiding trips, camping in, and exploring Rocky Mountain National Park. Because it has a special place in my heart, I decided it was a good place to begin this *National Park Mystery Series*.

I believe that the best way to care for our natural treasures is to first develop a deep connection with them. I hope you have been able to do so in these pages, and that you'll be able to get outside to develop an even deeper affection for the outdoors and national parks near you.

ACKNOWLEDGMENTS

First, I'd like to thank my daughters, India and Zion, who were the first to hear the story. They helped draft the cipher code in chapter two. My wife, Jenah, has supported this work from the beginning and believed in it. Susan Rosenbluth, my editing partner, is a Godsend. I'm so grateful to her for helping me sharpen my craft and create a more meaningful story. Kim Sheard did a fantastic job providing the first edit. Avery Simmons, my other editing partner, was so helpful in pointing out continuity breaks and providing ideas for how I could make both the dialogue and the story feel more authentic. I'm also grateful to Claire Gibson for her sharp eye for story and character development.

I'm deeply indebted to all of my beta-readers, especially Jeniece Trueman. Her feedback gave me the direction and the courage to rewrite the beginning of the book. Kirby Player has provided so much encouragement and fuel for my writing fire. I'm indebted to him for his expert knowledge and shared love for the national parks. I'd also like to thank my other beta readers: the Toth Family, Evan

Baribeau, Kezia Robb, Shera Moyer, Kristin Jardien, Annie Ice, Marianne McKiernan, Wilson Harwell, Anika Goyal, Alisha McDarris, Kathleen Barrett Kunau, Kate Brasch, and Kathleen McCubbin.

Author, Jonathan Rogers has been a wise and trusted guide. His writing workshops helped me get the momentum I needed to complete this project. (If you like adventure stories like this one, check out his Wilderking Trilogy).

I want to thank my launch team of educators, librarians, and national park lovers. If you'd like to join one of the launch teams for future books, you can sign up at: https://nationalparkmysteryseries.com/launchteam

I want to express my thanks to all the National Park Rangers and employees who have taken their time to serve our family.

Finally, I'd like to thank the ranger who helped plan my first weeklong trip in Rocky Mountain National Park. All I have on my 2004 backcountry permit are your initials: REN. Thank you.

IF YOU ENJOYED THE STORY...

If you enjoyed this story, I would appreciate your help getting copies into the hands of families and other young people. Here are a few ways you can do that:

- **Write a review** on Amazon and Goodreads.
- **Review Writing Tips:** A) Share your experience. What was it like for you to read and experience the story? B) It's a mystery, so try not to post any spoilers. C) If you read the book with a young person, describe what they enjoyed most about the story.
- **Upvote your favorite reviews.** On Amazon, you can *like* the reviews that you find most helpful. This helps to feature those reviews that best serve potential readers.

- **Loan** or give your copy to a friend.
- **Ask your local library** to acquire the series in their collection.
- **Purchase a copy.** They make great gifts. I'll be narrating the audiobooks, so look for those on my author page on audible: https://www. audible.com/author/Aaron-Johnson/ B086W2DTMT
- **Post on social media.** You can get links and images to post at https://nationalpark mysteryseries.com/launchteam
- **Share your copy with others.**
- **Connections**: I'd greatly appreciate it if you would connect me with people you know who may be able to help me promote the book and the series. You can make an introduction by emailing me at **aaron@ nationalparkmysteryseries.com**
- By the way, if you promote the books in some way, **email me** to let me know. As a way to say thank you, I've got a small gift to send your way.
- **Bulk Orders:** If you would like to place a bulk order at reduced pricing, reach out to me via email.

- **Speaking**: I would enjoy the opportunity to speak via Zoom or in-person with large and small groups. Wilson Rawls, author of *Where the Red Fern Grows*, spoke at thousands of schools. I hope to do the same.
- Visit https://nationalparkmysteryseries.com to discover more ways to engage with the series.

Into the Rainforest: Book 1 in the Lost City Series

https://NationalParkMysterySeries.com

I'd like to recommend a wonderful book written by my daughter, India Johnson. You can purchase a copy at Amazon at https://amzn.to/3KSj26D or search for Rebels' Daughter.

When twelve-year-old Sky sneaks out one night, her whole

world changes. On accident, she makes an enemy that will stop at nothing to destroy her family and humankind. Her parents are leaders of the rebellion, fighting against those who plan to enslave the last humans. That means that she has to be extra careful. Something she's not. Sky runs from talking wolves and crickcrawks, asking many questions about what's happening to her. Why are her things disappearing? Will she ever convince everyone that she can lead? And when something unexpected happens, she must face the most important question of all. Will she ever get home? Written by twelve-year-old (now fourteen) author, India Johnson, this is her first novel in the *Freedom Through Fire Saga*.

Proud Parent Note: India was the recipient of a Scholastic Art and Writing Regional Gold Key award for *The Rebels' Daughter*.

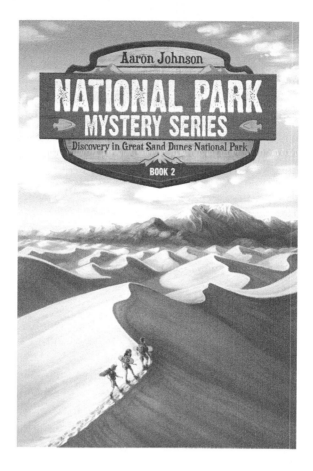

Book Preview

Discovery in Great Sand Dunes National Park
Scheduled for **Summer 2022** release.
You can download a longer book preview
and find updates at:
https://nationalparkmysteryseries.com

Chapter 1 - Summer 1880 - Sangre De Christo Mountains, Colorado

"Find that mutt and put it out of its misery." The man sat upon a black horse and wore a black overcoat with silver buttons. Though he was high in the mountains, his shirt and tie were crisp and unworn compared to the clothes of his two companions. A pair of hounds circled the three horses, baying and eager to pursue their prey.

"Yes, sir. The hounds have its scent now, so I expect we'll find it by sundown."

The third man patted the revolver strapped to his side. "And then we'll dispatch the critter."

"I expect to see you two back at the mine tomorrow," the well-dressed man said. He turned his horse and disappeared into the forest.

"Abigail!"

A girl of about sixteen appeared from behind the barn carrying two wooden buckets. Water sloshed over the rims of both, splashing a mix of dirt and water onto her dusty leather boots. The sweat on her forehead held fast several strands of strawberry blonde hair. A single braid swayed like a pendulum across the back of her button-up cotton shirt, which showed the unladylike signs of hard work. She set the buckets down on the steps of the house and tugged at the waistband of her denim jeans.

"Yes, ma'am."

"I wondered where you had gone off to, that's all." The short older woman folded her muscular arms across her chest. Like most ranchers, she looked older than her true age, having been weathered by the sun and toil. Her blue collared shirt was spotless thanks to the long apron she wore over her clothes.

"Mrs. Herard, could I take my horse out this afternoon when I'm finished with the chores?"

"Yes, you may, child. But don't go off too far. I'll need your help with dinner."

"Thank you, ma'am. I'll be back in time."

Abigail dragged several heavy rugs out of the ranch house and threw them over the clothesline to hit them with a wooden pitchfork. After sweeping and scrubbing the floors, she put the rugs back and then went to the barn to find her horse.

"Gideon, how are you, boy?" She ran her hand along the horse's side and then scratched his favorite spot, right between his eyes. Gideon was the last of her family. Abigail's parents and siblings had perished two years ago in the blizzard of 1878. She laid her cheek against his. "It's just you and me this afternoon, boy. We can do what we please until dinner." Abigail strapped a saddle on Gideon's back, slipped the bridle over his head, and led him out of the barn.

The vanilla scent of ponderosa pines filled the air, and the afternoon sun warmed Abigail's skin. She looked through the trees to the north, where the golden hills of the sand dunes spread out below them. Gideon made a nickering sound. "Not today, boy. We'll visit the dunes again soon enough. Today, we're going into the mountains." She put her foot in the stirrup and climbed into the saddle.

They made their way along the Medano Pass Road, which followed the creek up into the mountains toward Medano Pass. In the summer months, miners and settlers from the East used the road to cross the Sangre De Cristo Mountains.

Below the pass, Abigail steered Gideon off the road and onto a trail that led up and into the forest. Because the way was dense with fir and spruce trees, she had to duck under branches and then guide Gideon over deadfall and around the giant boulders that choked their path. An hour later, they arrived at their destination, Medano Lake.

Surrounded by mountains and snowfields, this alpine lake had become Abigail's favorite place in the world. Here, the only sounds came from the birds and the wind.

She tethered Gideon to a tree beside the water where he could drink, then walked across stepping stones to a boulder out in the lake. She sat down on the rock, wrapped her arms around her legs, and reveled in the beauty of the place. A breeze came down the mountainside and, like a spirit or the breath of God, jetted across the surface of the placid water.

A whimper interrupted the quiet. Gideon raised his head from the water and turned toward the sound. It came again, more of a cry this time. Abigail stood, turned to the woods behind her, and listened. Gideon watched with concern. She walked back across the stones to the shore of the lake, then followed the sounds into the forest. In a thicket of brush and briars, she found the source of the cries.

A golden retriever lay on its side. A gash across one of its front legs turned his yellow fur red with blood. "Oh, you poor boy," she said. "What happened to you?" The dog's muzzle and head were scratched by briars and its neck fur was matted with cockleburs.

She reached out her hand and touched his side. The dog whined, but he didn't snap. She studied his paws, all of them cracked and bleeding. "We need to get you some help."

His ears perked, and he turned his head to the north. Abigail turned to listen with him. From the ridge above the lake came the baying of hounds and the voices of men.